FURY OF MISFORTUNE

COREENE CALLAHAN

OliverHeberBooks

1

THE OUTSKIRTS — ABERDEEN, SCOTLAND

The tattoo gun buzzed as the needle punched into his skin.

Pain rippled up the inside of his forearm. Back flat to the padded table, Levin welcomed the raw nick and gnaw, using the burn to wipe away a different kind of hurt. The artist hunched over his arm shifted on his stool. Rubber wheels squeaked across the linoleum floor. Metal creaked, the sound loud in the near silence, broadcasting the human's nervousness.

Levin didn't blame him.

He wasn't the male's usual client, easy to please, patient during the process. A dragon warrior with lethal skill, he was exacting. Cold. Merciless. Could even be cruel if he didn't get what he wanted. And he wanted the tattoo to be perfect. Needed it almost as much as the ice magic rumbling in his veins.

He might pride himself on being controlled, but one slip of the ink gun, a single missed stroke or shaky line, and he'd KO the motherfucker. Slice his head from his neck with a murmur. Rip his heart out through his chest. Leave the human in a messy pile on the shop floor in the middle of the night, under the glow of neon light, and never look back.

Unfair, perhaps, but...

He hadn't brought his drawing—the one he'd labored and obsessed over for days—to the most talented tattoo artist in Scotland for nothing. Word on the street said the male had skills. How much remained to be seen, as Levin hadn't looked down at the ink yet, but…

It had better be perfect when finished. Absolutely *perfect*. An exact replica of the face he saw in his dreams every day.

Goddess. That face.

A total fucking mystery.

One he hated almost as much as he loved closing his eyes each morning, knowing she'd visit him while he slept. A vision in white, brown skin glowing with vitality, dark eyes shining with intelligence and mischief.

The needle jabbed across the inside of his wrist.

Another round of pain sheeted through him. He clenched his teeth, then closed his eyes, allowing the caustic energy to flow through him before releasing it. His nostrils flared. A soft thud sounded. The rustle of denim. The creak of a leather jacket.

Levin waited for curiosity to get the better of his brothers-in-arms. For the interrogation to begin. For the comments to start.

Boot soles brushed over the stained floor. A shadow fell over him and the table a second before—

"Who is she?" Deep voice. Soft tone tied to strings of intense interest.

"None of yer business, Ran."

Rannock, his wing-mate for the night, ignored the quiet warning. "Where'd you meet her?"

"What'd I say?"

"I'm choosing tae ignore yer bullshite," Rannock said, coming around the head of the table. "Why didnae you bring her home?"

"Ran—"

"Spill, Lev. You know I'll not let it go if for no other reason than Cate will pester me until I find out."

"Shite." Levin twitched as the needle hit a sensitive spot. "Ye're being led around by yer dick. Pussy-whipped."

"Absolutely. Best way tae be, mon," Rannock said. "My female rocks my world in bed."

"Or the kitchen." The third member of his happy crew tonight, Tempel laughed. "Caught you coming out of the hall closet yesterday too."

Rannock grinned. "I take her wherever she wants me."

"Which is everywhere," Tempel said, green eyes sparkling with humor from his perch on the chipped countertop across the room.

Leaning in for a closer look at his arm, Rannock shrugged. "What can I say, mon, I'm blessed."

Levin sighed. "Fucking hell."

"Stop stalling, Lev." Shifting on his perch, Tempel planted his forearms on the tops of his thighs, all humor gone, a serious expression replacing the amused one on his face. "What's bothering you?"

"Nothing."

Rannock growled. "Donnae do that."

"What?"

"Treat us like we're stupid." Bronze eyes leveled on him, Rannock crossed his arms. He rocked back on his heels, then tipped his chin at the human inking the female's face into his Levin's skin. "She's important tae you. You wouldn't be here, doing what you're doing, otherwise."

Levin clenched his teeth.

Goddamn his packmates. None of the warriors he lived, trained, and fought with respected boundaries. As a group, they busted through every barrier he put up, asking questions Levin wanted to leave unanswered. He disliked sharing. Hated vulnerability in all its varied shades. Admitting to weakness rubbed him the wrong way. Not that his brothers cared. The males never let anything go, poking, prodding, pushing for the truth.

"Levin." Rannock's voice snapped through the quiet.

His throat tightened. "I haven't actually met her."

Rannock blinked. "Not once?"

"Never?" Tempel's dark brows popped toward his forehead. "You don't know who she is?"

Staring at the rough planked ceiling, Levin shook his head.

Rannock made a sound of disbelief. "Mayhap you've seen her at the pub."

"Or out on patrol…in passing," Tempel said. "Edinburgh, maybe?"

"I'd have remembered." One hundred percent accurate. He wasn't blowing smoke. Nothing about her was forgettable.

"You've been distracted lately." Boots swinging in the breeze, Tempel banged his heels into cabinets. "Got lots on your plate."

Wasn't that the fucking truth?

He had so many balls in the air. The Danes moving into Scottish territory, attacking at random. The Archguard arseholes messing with his pack. Trying to figure out who wanted the new innkeeper at The White Hare dead. So many problems to solve, tons of intel yet to be gathered. His specialty. He moved in shadowy circles, rubbing shoulders with the worse Magickind had to offer, still…

The artist moved onto another section, needling over a new patch of skin.

Levin flexed his hand. "No way I would've missed her."

Not *her*.

Her aura was too distinctive. A siren's song, calling to him with the chilly, jewel-like energy she wore like a second skin. He more than sensed her in the dreamscape. He *felt* her, his dragon half so attuned he ached with need every afternoon when he woke up.

"You gotta figure out who she is, Lev," Tempel said.

"I'm not sure she's real. Could be naught more than a figment of my imagination." Hopes. Dreams. Deep yearning. Levin's dragon half's way of telling him he longed to find and claim his mate. "A phantom come tae haunt my dreams."

"Nay, brother. Ye're hypersensitive tae cosmic shifts. If ye're dreaming of her, you've locked on tae something important." Menace shimmering like a cloud around him, Rannock leaned closer. Fear spiked in the artist's scent. The male twitched. His friend stepped back, giving the artist more breathing room, aware Levin would kill him if the human's hand slipped. Orange-bronze gaze full of laughter, he flicked his fingers, gesturing to the tattoo. "Gorgeous design."

"Aye." Though *gorgeous* lacked a certain something.

He liked *captivating* better. The tattoo was a masterpiece of black and gray gradient. An exact depiction of a stunning face framed by thick braids inside a dragon skull with hollowed-out eye sockets, Viking horns rising in a twist from bare bone.

"You draw it?"

He tipped his chin.

With a grunt, Tempel hopped off his perch. "She might be in trouble. Sending up smoke signals, requesting your help."

His attention snapped toward the newest member of the Scottish pack. Rescued from a Dragonkind prison and brought home by Vyroth, Tempel was almost as big a pest as Rannock. An earth dragon with vicious inclinations, the American loved to dig. In the dirt, sure, but he also enjoyed a good puzzle. The more intricate the mystery, the harder Tempel worked to solve it.

"Details, man." Cracking his scarred knuckles,

Tempel strode across the shop. His boots thumped. Sharp bio-energy twisted around him as his focus sharpened. "Anything consistent—time, place, circumstance? Any pattern you can see?"

Levin shook his head. He wished there was clear pattern, but he'd already analyzed his dreams. Thought of all the possibilities. Run down every clue provided. Day after day while he slept. Traveling great distances in his mind. Chasing her though blowing snow and across icy plains, coming up empty, never managing to reach her.

"Nothing concrete tae guide me." The needle traveled over an already sore spot. Levin shifted on the table, mind on the mystery, not the human inking him. "She comes tae me in the ice and snow. Walking toward me across the tundra. She whispers tae me in a language I donnae understand."

"Odd," Rannock murmured as the ink gun stopped buzzing.

The pressure eased, then left Levin's arm. Intense pain lightened to a harsh sting.

"The worse sort of mind-fuck," he said, tensing as the artist wiped the tattoo, spreading cold gel over his inked skin.

Rannock hummed.

The quiet thump of combat boots stopped beside the table. Green eyes full of concern, Tempel met his gaze. "Levin, I've seen this before. My uncle, Ezram, had dreams. Intense. Brutal. Premonitions he couldn't control and never—"

The cell phone Levin hated, but carried anyway, chirped in his pocket.

He glanced at the artist. "You done?"

The male's throat bobbed as he nodded, the movement jerky with fear.

Only then did Levin look down, and—

Air left his lungs on a rush. Goddess. There she was,

the female he'd never met, but couldn't get out of his head. Dark hair. Thick eyelashes. Incredible face with just the right intensity staring out at him from inside a raw-bone dragon skull. From the surface of his own skin.

His chest tightened.

Thank Christ, thank Christ, thank Christ.

He owned a piece of her now. Something to hold on to, a way to see her every night, a way to connect with her during his waking hours.

Unable to speak, he called on his magic. A fold of bills materialized in his palm. Tossing the money onto the tray next to the human, he nodded his approval and rolled off the table.

His boots hit the floor.

The artist released the breath he'd been holding.

"Lev—"

"Leave it be, Ran."

His friend stared at him, gaze drilling into his, then tipped his chin. "For now."

"Forever." Putting his feet in gear, Levin reached for his cell phone. As he pulled it from the back pocket of his jeans, he headed for the front door.

The iPhone pinged again.

Halfway across the one-room tattoo shop, he punched in the passcode with his mind. The screen went from black to bright, revealing two text messages from one of his sources. A confidential informant, a werewolf who acted less like a warrior and more like a drama queen with every week that passed.

His eyes narrowed on the message. Fucking Shell. Total pain in the arse, and yet he refused to cut the wolf loose. No matter how annoying, the male owed him, working hard to unearth information Levin might find useful to pay off his debt...and stay on the Scottish pack's good side.

Sometimes the information Shell provided ended up being useful. Other times, it was pure shite.

The way of the world he inhabited. Subterfuge and obfuscation were par for the course while wading through the dredges of Magickind. One never knew when a CI would hit pay dirt and provide the interesting information. Something Levin needed on multiple fronts, given the Danes had upped their game, attacking human settlements close to Aberdeen, and a splinter group of Druids had surfaced, threatening the inn he and his pack now protected.

A third text flashed across his phone.

"Fuck."

"What?" Tempel asked, bumping his shoulder.

Levin glanced at his friend. "Shell."

"Shite." Ahead of him, halfway to the door, Rannock glanced over his shoulder. "Tell me we donnae have tae meet that bampot tonight?"

He read Shell's text messages again.

SOS
Nellfield Cemetery.
10 mins.

THE WORDS RANG THROUGH HIM. Shite. As much as he wanted to, he couldn't ignore the message. Despite his contrary personality, the werewolf sometimes stumbled on actionable intel. Frustration made him clench his teeth. Duty kept him moving toward the door, even though he knew the chances the information Shell had unearthed would end up being long shot. Pure folly. The kind that would put him out on a limb, but in order to be sure, he needed to meet the male—sift through the shite the wolf shoveled his way and separate fact from fiction.

An arduous task. One he didn't enjoy, but…

Leaving his CI hanging wasn't a good idea.

"Hate tae say it, lads, but we're making a detour," he said, knowing the pronouncement would piss off his packmates. The grumbles proved it, but Levin held the line. He wanted to shift into dragon form and get out into open skies too, begin the hunt by getting out on patrol and shut the Danes down, but the wolf needed some of his attention first. "Shell sounds scared. He might be onto something."

Tempel grunted. "You put him on the Druids?"

"That and unearthing the location of the Danish lair."

"Do you think Grizgunn would let that info leak?" Tempel asked, referring to the Danish commander. "Is he really that stupid?"

"Nay," Levin said, being honest, refusing to indulge false hope. "But I cannae discount Shell. The wolf's good at worming his way into places he doesnae belong. Might prove fruitful."

"Hope so," Rannock said. "I wanna blow Grizgunn out the sky, but I'll settle for burying him alive inside his lair."

Tempel snarled in agreement.

Lengthening his stride, Levin upped his pace. He needed to get to Nellfield Cemetery fast. Shell might be a drama queen, but he'd never used an *SOS* before. Something was wrong. Off in ways Levin sensed drifting on the open air. The smell. The taste. The twang of powerful magic he hadn't yet placed. All of it pointed to trouble, falling like dominos, scraping across his instincts, sending intuition spiking. Might be nothing. Could prove to be more than the usual sinister. With the werewolf in play, anything was possible.

2

Night air tickling his senses, Levin angled his wings into the wind. Fast flight slowed to smooth glide as city lights winked through tangled clouds. Warm air rushed over his temples. The horns rising from the crown of his head vibrated as his sonar pinged. The ice coating his blue, white, and gray tiger-striped scales cracked, then shattered, flying out behind him. Frost chips peppered building tops, striking rain-streaked windowpanes like automatic gun fire.

Bronze scales flashing in the gloom, Rannock swerved to avoid getting hit by the barrage. His mouth kept pace, pushing a complaint through mind-speak. *"Slow down, mon. You trying tae kill me?"*

Another sheet of ice flew off his flank.

"Shite." Rannock dodged again, wings seesawing above the skyline. *"Power down."*

"No time," Levin said, scanning the ground, searching for Nellfield Cemetery in the twist of sepia-tone streets.

"Plenty of time," Rannock said with a huff. *"We're less than two minutes away."*

Levin didn't answer. He tightened the cloaking spell hiding him from human eyes instead. Snow and ice funneled into a cyclone behind him.

Rannock grumbled something obscene under his breath.

Flying off his right wingtip, Tempel snorted in amusement.

Levin flicked the tip of his tail. Razor-sharp spikes rattled. More ice shards flew, smashing into the side of an apartment tower. He heard human feet hit the floor. Lights inside a cluster of granite clad buildings flipped on. Curtains moved enough for pale, sleepy faces to peer out their windows. Without slowing, he sliced between two towers. The ground shook. More condo occupants peered out from behind glass panes, no doubt curious about the sudden appearance of winter while in the throes of the warmest spring in history.

"Lev," Rannock said, flipping up and over, avoiding a face-full of snow.

Levin shook his head. *"Shell won't wait. He'll rabbit if I donnae—"*

"Doubtful," Tempel murmured, doing the unthinkable—agreeing with Rannock.

An important occasion to note, given Tempel argued more with Rannock than anyone else in the pack. Usually, it had to do with a sporting event. Sometimes, though, he pushed Rannock's buttons for fun, instigating a fight, wanting to brawl. Crazy by anyone's standards, but Levin approved. As a bronze dragon, his friend needed the outlet, to draw blood more than most males. The fact the earth dragon met—and more than matched—one of the most brutal Dragonkind warriors in existence said good things about the American.

"You donnae know Shell." Urgency riding him hard, Levin upped the pace. Wind whistled off his wingtips, shrieking into contrails behind him. *"He's flighty."*

"Don't need to know him," Tempel said, shrugging massive shoulders. Green and brown scales flecked by gold clicked. Levin eyeballed the male, marveling at the

size of him. Tempel was jacked—bigger than both him and Rannock, with the kind of vicious intensity that made other Dragonkind turn tail and fly in the opposite direction. *"Short text, but the wolf sounded scared. He won't rabbit."*

Levin grunted, but kept his eye on the prize.

Less than a minute away, Nellfield Cemetery rose like a beacon in the near dark. Large, grassy expanses contained by a high wall. Narrow pathways lit by the faint glow of garden lights meandering between clusters of ancient trees. And tombstones. So many tombstones worn smooth by bitter Highland weather, blunt faces awaiting the next wave of daytime visitors.

Typical. Nothing unusual about the setup, except…

Gaze anchored to the ground, Levin frowned. Something about the graveyard felt off. Wrong in ways he couldn't quite pin down. The odd scent wafting on the breeze, maybe. The claw and scrub of intuition, perhaps. Couple that with his experience running countless covert ops for his pack and…aye. Nellfield Cemetery wasn't his friend tonight.

Not that the source of his disquiet mattered.

Smart or not, he was going in to pull the information out of Shell.

Descending another hundred feet, Levin lined up his approach, putting the graveyard in his cross hairs. Magic rolled like artic winds in front of him, invisible shards whipping down cobblestone streets like snow across frozen tundra. He drew on the threads, sifting through scent and sound, and…

There.

Right fucking *there*—a keen sense of something twisted. Wild. Potent. Unpredictable. A scent combination he couldn't read, but as the redolent twang knocked on memory's door, his eyes narrowed. Seconds away from landing, he flexed his talons. Sharpened to lethal points, his claws pricked the centers of his palms. The nick and gnaw settled him. The smells began to separate—the odor of human groundkeepers, a heavy dose of werewolf on the wind and…an odd vibration.

Trace energy. Almost scentless, but not quite. An essence that wasn't native to the Highlands, or the city he called home.

Caution urged him into a holding pattern. One rotation turned into two. Floating in the seam of a strong northeasterly, he banked into a sweeping turn and—

"*Shite*," Rannock muttered, sensing the disturbance too.

Flying off his wingtip, Tempel bumped him with the side of his spiked tail. A love tap, just enough to get his attention, but he received the silent warning the American conveyed.

He threw his packmate a sideways glance. *"What?"*

"You don't smell it?"

"Aye, but I cannae place it. Do you—"

"Savannah. Deep in the earth." Green eyes shimmering, Tempel flexed huge talons. Scaled knuckles scarred by years of digging cracked, broadcasting his unease. *"Remember when I burrowed into the—"*

"Fuck," Levin muttered. Details drew a straight line from the East Coast of the United States six months ago to here and now. *"The Witch's Cauldron."*

"Yeah," Tempel said. *"Whatever's down there has shades of her."*

"Just my luck," Rannock muttered. *"Goddamn witch nearly killed me."*

Shades of her.

The words banged around inside his head. A bad taste washed into his mouth. Savannah hadn't been fun. Necessary, sure, but not fun, given Rannock almost died while protecting his mate. Bright, beautiful, irrepressible, Cate had come through with flying colors. Rannock still suffered from the near-miss, becoming so overprotective Cate threatened to smother him with a pillow while he slept once a week.

Levin didn't blame her.

He couldn't blame Rannock either.

The events in America held all the markers of messed-up. An experience no one wanted to repeat or relive.

Moments from putting paws to pavement, Levin reshuffled his deck, flipping through the plays he employed when meeting a confidential informant. Strategy shifted, coalescing into a more cohesive plan. Landing inside the cemetery would be easier, more expedient. The method of drop-in he usually used when dealing with Shell. Scaring the shite out of the skittish werewolf worked best most of the time, but…

Not tonight.

A more considered approach was needed. Which meant he wouldn't be dropping into Nellfield Cemetery. Not until he understood what awaited him between the tombstones.

"Post up, lads." Monitoring the cobble-lined streets, Levin picked his spot. The spikes riding his spine rattled as he descended, preparing to land hard and fast. Annoyance flared. Fucking Shell. Always so much trouble. Giving the werewolf his time and attention had been a mistake. He'd known the male would become a problem the instant the bastard crossed his path. *"Outside the three-mile marker. I'm going in alone."*

Rannock bared his fangs.

Tempel shook his head. *"Not a good idea."*

"I don't want tae spook Shell…or give whoever's with him reason tae run."

Rannock grunted. *"Might be a setup."*

Good point. But nothing Levin hadn't already considered. *"If things go sideways, you and Tempel will be close enough tae cover me."*

"Donnae mess around, Lev." Treating him to a load of

stink-eye, Rannock clipped him with the bronze hook tipping his wing. Metal shrieked along his side, drawing a line across his frost-covered scales. Sparks flew. Snowflakes melted, turning into raindrops in his wake. *"Mind-speak stays open. We need tae hear everything said down there. I donnae care what information the rank bastard has—if I think ye're about tae be fucked, I'll fly in and rip the wolf's head off."*

"Might improve yer mood," Levin said, shrugging off the sting to his ribs. *"For once."*

"Yers too. You never liked Shell."

"True."

Tempel bared his fangs. *"You two done fucking around?"*

"Temp—"

"No joke, Lev. Get the intel and get out."

A curl of amusement swept through him. *"Okay, Mum."*

Venomous mist shot from his nostrils as Tempel huffed. *"Fuck off."*

"Love you too," Levin said, flashing dual-bladed canines.

The big American sighed.

A nasty glint in his eyes, Rannock shook his head.

Levin folded his wings, dropping between his wing-mates. No sense putting it off, or circling one more time. He had an idea of what awaited him. Not a good one, but the intel wouldn't collect itself. The cemetery might not be ideal for this kind of meet, but he couldn't back out now. Not with curiosity running rampant and killer instincts tingling.

Cold air swirled as he touched down softly, without his claws making a snick of sound on rough cobble-stones. Hidden inside a cloaking spell, he settled into a low crouch in the middle of the deserted street. Frost gathered beneath his paws, then spread across stone as he drew a deep breath. He held it until his lungs burned, then let it go.

The icy exhale streamed between his fangs. Magic tumbled, hitting the raised curb, splashing up and over the wall surrounding the cemetery. Uncovered in the rush, the bad vibration turned to sinister shimmer, undulating like fire in the weave of invisibility.

Levin watched the light show a moment, then shifted into human form.

With a murmur, he conjured his clothes. Faded jeans, plain white t-shirt, his favorite leather jacket settled against his skin. He didn't bother with boots. As an ice dragon, bare soles worked best for him. The chill would keep him calm in the face of whatever idiocy Shell planned to dish out.

Putting himself in gear, he strode out of the street. Fog wreathed, tumbling over the tops of his feet as he stepped onto the sidewalk. The cold deepened. The quiet expanded. The darkness enveloped him, cradling him in her arms, welcoming him like a native son. His dragon half tapped into the bad vibration. Images flashed across his mental screen. Blurry and indistinct. Dull and colorless. Swirling grays, the space between the known and unknown. A premonition. A well-timed warning. Pure power as aggression sparked, pushing the need to annihilate through his veins.

Light vanquished the dark as his eyes began to glow. White shimmer tinged by blue washed through the gloom. Shadows moved from black shapes to knowable objects. Details crystalized—the grainy texture of granite blocks, the dark green of spiked tree leaves, thick branches leaning over the wall above his head, the velvet petals of blood-red roses in the courtyard across the street.

Sliding deeper into the shadows, Levin scanned his surroundings again. Quiet neighborhood. Narrow, curving street. The low hum of electrical interference in the air. No movement in the alleyways. No humans out for a midnight stroll. Nothing but a tidy row of parked cars and shuttered windows staring out from the face of the three-story building opposite him.

"*In position,*" he murmured, pushing the words through the connection he shared with his brothers-in-arms. "*Anything?*"

"*All quiet.*" Claws scraped against metal as Rannock shifted on his chosen perch. "*No rogues in the area.*"

"*Tempel?*"

A clamor came through mind-speak. Sounded like a jackhammer, but Levin knew better. He clenched his teeth to keep from laughing. Jesus. Earth dragons. He should've known. The male wasn't like Rannock. As a Metallic, Rannock grounded himself with metal, choosing to perch on steel shingles. Tempel, on the other hand, burrowed every chance he got, preferring dirt to sky most nights.

"*The stink is in the air, not underground,*" Tempel said, the calamity assaulting Levin's senses, making his mind shudder. "*You're clear.*"

Well, all right, then. Go time.

"*Stand by. I'm going in,*" Levin said, indulging in a final shoulder check.

Nothing and nobody.

Returning his gaze on the curved top of the wall, he hopped the ten-foot barrier. Heavy mist swirled like a cape behind him. Thorn bushes grabbed at his pant legs. Mortar in need of repair crumbled under his hand, sprinkling the ground as he cleared a hedge and landed on the other side without making a sound.

On his haunches in the V of two raised tree roots, he gathered more gloom and absorbed the stillness. Stacks of quiet. Layers of nothingness, swirling like acid, sliding against and burning into each other. An unnatural raptorial buzz assaulting the silence, nearly imperceptible, but not quite.

He tightened his focus. His sonar pinged, dropping a net over the graveyard. He pulled on individual strings, filtering through filaments of information. Two blips appeared on his mental screen. A picture formed in his mind's eye. Two males standing close, the taller one behind the other, the shorter one quivering in fear.

Shell—caught, trapped, at the mercy of another male.

Pushing to his feet, Levin turned toward the signal. Three hundred yards to his right, in the inner sanctum of the cemetery. Amid the tangle of crooked pathways, stone crypts, and tall, elaborate headstones. A place he knew well. He'd visited the section more than once, providing Tydrin with cover when his brother-in-arms brought his mate, Ivy, to visit her parents' graves.

Suspicion slithered into view, prompting an important question. Was the meeting place a coincidence, or a detail he needed to pay attention to?

The location suggested the latter.

Whoever held Shell captive must know his pack frequented the cemetery. Which meant the bastard possessed inside information. The kind that might prove dangerous to him and his brothers-in-arms.

A low growl escaped him. Cracking his knuckles, hoping for a fight, he moved around the massive oak. The night air split open, allowing him to hear what no human ever would. He tilted his head and breathed in, cycling through the different scents. Old leaves. Fresh flowers. The tang of decaying flesh unpinned by overturned, damp loam and—

"*Shite,*" he said under his breath.

"*What?*" Rannock growled.

"*Vampire, but worse.*"

"*What's worse than a vampire?*" The clamor and bang died, sliding into silence as Tempel stopped digging.

"*One that doesn't smell right,*" Levin said, disbelief

warring with certainty. He battled a second, logic arguing with instinct, but—

"*Illness, mayhap?*" Rannock asked. "*There's been a rash of unexplained—*"

"*Nay. 'Tisn't the blood sickness plaguing the vampire population of late,*" he said, wanting to deny what his dragon half already knew, but...what good would that do? He couldn't wish away—or mistake—the repugnant scent. *Vampire* tinged by the essence of ancient Fae. A combination that shouldn't exist, never mind be shimmering with the promise of violence so close to the lair he and his brothers called home. "*Powerful. A hybrid, mayhap.*"

"*It's already gone sideways.*" Metal shrieked as Rannock prepared to leave his perch. "*Levin—two choices. Haul yer arse outta there, or I'm flying in.*"

"*Let me get the lay of the land, Ran. I wanna lay eyes on the bastard.*"

"*And the wolf?*" Tempel asked, voicing a legitimate concern.

Levin bit down on a curse.

The werewolf was a pain in the arse, no question, and yet, even knowing he should, Levin refused to cut him loose. After months of meeting the idiot at all hours of the night, somehow, he'd ended up feeling responsible for the wolf. The wrong reaction, given Shell never acted responsibly. He showed up to every meeting stoned, drunk, or both. No doubt one of the reasons he managed to get good intel. No one considered Shell a threat. Or realized he was listening while pretending to be passed out in a pool of his own piss.

Levin ought to feel bad about the state of the male. Getting the wolf help would be better than paying his fees, than watching the bastard use the money to kill himself inch by slow inch. Reality, though, was a capricious bitch, reminding Levin what he already knew. Nothing he did, or said, would move Shell onto a healthier path. A person must first admit to having a problem—and accept help—for true change to occur.

Cold to the core, his dragon half agreed with the maxim, refusing to let him take ownership of Shell's decline. He didn't buy the werewolf drugs...or inject the shite into the male's veins. He traded money for information. Something Shell excelled at delivering—even when he was high as a fucking kite.

Still...

A good male would shut down the money train until the werewolf got sober. A better one would stop taking Shell's calls altogether, make it clear he had other informants who offered reliable information without the added drama.

Releasing a pent-up breath, Levin pinged his pack-mates. *"Moving. A hundred yards out. You got me?"*

"Tracking," Rannock murmured.

Tempel hummed. *"In position."*

Dragon senses roaming, Levin slipped through a break in a tall hedge and traversed a narrow path. His bare soles whispered over a compact dirt. Twin pillars guarding the inner sanctum came into view. Stone-faced gargoyles peered down from the tops of the columns, welcoming him in, urging him forward.

The scent of vampire strengthened. The shadows cast by old growth trees deepened.

His night vision sharpened, allowing him to see fine details as he moved between headstones. Crumbling stone Goliaths in the oldest section of the graveyard. Sculpted monoliths choked by vines, long forgotten by those who spent their days burying the dead. He turned right, moving past an ornate garden gate. Acrid stench radiated out in concentric circles, joining the smell of bluebells growing along the path.

The gate waved closed behind him. Rusty hinges creaked.

Bilious yellow fog seeped from holes cut into the

turf. Abnormal, rough-edged, shallow wounds that suggested cruelty and spoke of an unchecked temper. His upper lip curled, baring one of his canines. Fucking vampires. Unnatural bastards. A curse upon Magickind, a scourged released upon the earth, one Dragonkind needed to take more seriously.

Keeping the vampire horde in check had always been his kind's responsibility. Magickind's hierarchy put the cultural precepts in place centuries ago. Dragonkind sat at the top of the food chain, often being asked to police other magic-bound species and protect the weaker races from unwarranted attacks. In some places, the strategy worked. In other places, it didn't. Policing depended on the region...and the male in command of the dragon warriors in his pack. A strong commander kept the peace, operating under the guiding principles handed down by the Goddess of All Things. A sadistic one preyed on others, hunting weaker species for sport.

A disgusting practice. One the Archguard needed to shut down, but never would. The useless bastards in Prague turned a blind eye, refusing to interfere in pack politics and practices unless it somehow benefited the five dynastic families who ruled Dragonkind. Power was the name of the game. And Rodin (leader of the Archguard) played it very well.

Which meant the Scottish pack was on its own, isolated from other packs by geography, left alone to police their territory and shield those in need of protection. But the vampires? Levin gritted his teeth. The recent vampire migration to the Highlands needed to be addressed before it got out of hand. Before the hunting reached dangerous heights and someone died.

Left to their own devices, the greedy bloodsuckers would destabilize the region. Hurt the human population his pack protected while out on patrol every night, so...

Time to quit stalling and face the music.

A conversation with Cyprus was in order. His commander needed to be briefed and brought up to speed. A task Levin didn't relish, but for which he was uniquely suited.

As his pack's intel officer, he moved in shadowy circles, keeping his finger on the pulse of Magickind. With Kruger's mate, Ferguson (innkeeper of The White Hare) in the fold, his job had gotten easier. Through her, he tracked the number of Magickind coming and going from the territory his pack ruled.

The number of vampires staying at the inn had tripled in recent months. Some had grown sick and died. Others continued to thrive. A puzzle. More than a touch concerning, given none of the bastards seemed to be leaving. They lived (or died) inside the Parkland, on the grounds of The White Hare.

"Levin, you alive down there?" Rannock asked, throwing attitude from three miles away. *"I donnae hear anything."*

"Chill, mon." Levin's nose twitched as the noxious smell of vampire increased. He paused between crypts with Greek keys chiseled into their stone faces. His magic uncoiled. Ice swirled, frosting his skin, freezing wildflowers along the path into a death pose. He ignored the environmental fallout and tilted his head, listening for signs of movement. *"I'm almost there."*

Turning at an intersection, he stepped into an enclave surrounded by towering tombstones. Two males stood in shadow, beyond the patch of moonlight less than ten feet away. Sensing his arrival, but unable to see him, the vampire shifted, moving Shell front and center, tightening his grip around the werewolf's throat, using him as a living shield.

"I know you're here." A soft voice carrying shades of the American South—melodic, designed to hypnotize.

A trait all vampires owned and wielded without effort. "Show yourself."

Levin considered denying the bastard, but...

He wouldn't get the information he needed if he allowed instinct its head and stabbed the vampire with an ice dagger. *Talk first, kill later.* Sounded like a plan, even if he'd prefer to extract the intel by putting the arsehole's head in a vise and squeezing it out of him.

"Levin," Shell rasped, chest rising and fall too fast.

With a flick of his fingers, Levin dropped the invisibility spell, allowing the pair to see him.

The vampire blinked. "Big fucker, aren't you?"

"Size matters," Levin murmured, flexing his hands. His knuckles cracked. Sharp snaps rippled through the clearing, a sound that spoke of fury, the gesture designed to do one thing—intimidate.

The vampire didn't mistake him. His mouth curved, amusement easy to read in the lines of his face. Brave, really. A trait Levin normally admired in another. Courage was, after all, rare. Most males turned belly up when faced with him. Shell's captor stood strong, seemingly unconcerned by the vicious vibe Levin threw off like pheromones.

Gaze riveted to the male, Levin walked toward the pair.

"Stop," the vampire said. "That's close enough."

Taking another step, he raised a brow. "Or what?"

"Shell loses his head."

The werewolf whimpered.

Levin stopped in the middle of the clearing. "You wanted me here. I'm here. Let him go."

"You know, I don't think I will, though..." The vampire trailed off, his tone full of false consideration. "You give me what I want, I'll consider it."

"Bullshite," he murmured, studying the vampire. "He's dead either way."

Fear in his scent, Shell met his gaze. "Levin, you need to—"

"Now, now, wolf," the bastard whispered, voice imbued with magic—mind control wielded with stunning efficiency. "Remember what we talked about?"

The werewolf's face paled a second before his eyes glazed over, and he slipped back under the vampire's control.

"There's a good boy." The bastard smiled, exposing a row of needle-sharp teeth. He stepped forward, pushing Shell into the moonlight. The weak glow fell, dappling the planes of his face. "Shell doesn't have to die, dragon. Whether he does or not is entirely up to you."

Staring at him, Levin felt his brows collide.

That voice. That face. Something about both sat on the tip of his brain, within reach as he ran his gaze over the male holding his CI captive. Blond hair. Light blue eyes alive with excitement. Excellent bone structure, the kind that made females pause and take a second look. Six feet tall with a trim physique that hinted at power, suggesting the vampire knew how to handle himself in a fight and...

Fucking hell.

He recognized the bastard.

"Henry Biscayne," he said, keeping his stance relaxed.

"Surprise," Henry murmured, pale eyes alight with fierce pleasure.

"*Shit,*" Tempel growled.

"*Fuck,*" Rannock said at the same time. Scales clicked together. The sound of flapping wings came through the link. "*Airborne. Ninety seconds out.*"

Levin didn't answer. He kept his eyes trained on the male who'd died of magic poisoning after being tortured by the Blind Witch inside The Witch's Cauldron six months ago. The fact Henry stood in the Highlands, changed from human to magical abomination, was more than surprising—it was incomprehensible. The bastard should be dead. Levin had watched Rannock dig the grave, and Cate (Henry's daughter) bury her sire inside a cemetery in Savannah, Georgia, with a triad of Shadow Walkers' blessing.

Shelving his shock, Levin raised a brow. "You rang?"

"So cocky," Henry said, flexing his hand. Long, pointed fingernails dented the skin over Shell's jugular. Mind blank, body still responsive, the werewolf flinched. The vampire grinned, reveling in his hostage's pain. "The wolf seems to think you value him. Is that true?"

Was it?

Good question. The truth painted with bright colors, but also in shades of gray. And those shades told him Shell had outlived his usefulness. Still…

Did he really want to see the werewolf dead?

"Did you know?" Henry asked conversationally, as though he had all the time in the world. As though Levin wasn't about to cut him in half. As though Rannock and Tempel weren't moving in for the kill. "I haven't yet tasted werewolf. What do you think, Shell? Should we give it a try?"

"What do you want?" Levin growled, losing patience.

"Call off your crew first. I know you're not here alone. Something I've learned during my time in Scotland—dragons travel and hunt in packs. Smart practice, all things considered, but you see…" Henry paused for dramatic effect. Bloodsuckers loved theatrics. The more shocking, the better the bastards liked it. "The wolf and I are now of one mind, aren't we, Shell? Call them off, or the information you seek dies with him and stays with me."

Fighting Henry's control, Shell stared at him, tears in his eyes. "Levin, I'm sorry. I never meant for—"

"Quiet," Henry said, strangling Shell's voice. "Decide, dragon. What's it to be—the information you need to kill the Danes, or a dead werewolf?"

The Danes.

What the fuck did that mean? What had Shell dug up? What information did Biscayne now hold?

Interest shimmered through Levin. Intense excitement followed. He reached for control, refusing to show his hand. Intuition warned him the intel Biscayne had might prove pivotal. Whatever he knew could turn the tide, giving the Scottish pack the upper hand in the war they fought against the Danes.

Levin wanted the intel. Needed it much more than he wanted to keep Shell alive.

Tension flickered along his spine. Gaze boring into Biscayne's, he murmured, "Hold."

With a curse, Rannock put on the brakes. High winds hissed through the link as Tempel stopped digging.

The crackle in the air moved from high whine to low buzz.

Tapped into the frequency, Biscayne smiled. "That wasn't so hard, was it?"

"You've got sixty seconds," Levin said. "Make good use of it, vamp."

Unfazed by the insult, the bastard chuckled.

Levin flexed his hands. "Biscayne—"

"I know where Grizgunn sleeps."

The revelation hammered into him, striking so deep Levin tensed as the shock wave struck. His fingertips started to tingle. The fine hairs on the back of his neck stood on end. He swallowed a low snarl.

The Danish lair.

He and his brothers had been searching for months without any luck. No matter what strategy the Scottish pack employed, the Danes managed to stay one step ahead. But if he knew where the enemy slept, he'd hold all the cards. Be able to plan an attack, kill the rogues in a single stroke, eliminate the threat to the warriors he considered his brothers. His packmates meant everything to him—family, security, acceptance. He'd do whatever it took to protect them, along with the females who now lived inside his pack's fold.

Seeing his reaction, Henry chuckled. "Thought that might interest you."

"Where?"

"No so fast, dragon, I've got—"

"Where?" Levin said, walking deeper into the clearing.

Dragging Shell backward, Henry retreated toward a tombstone. He stopped when Levin did.

"Tell me, Biscayne."

"I have a few demands."

"List them."

"My butterflies—Nicole and Cate," Henry said. "Bring both to The White Hare. Simple exchange—my daughters for the Dane's location."

Rannock snarled. *"No fucking way."*

"I'm going to tear the asshole in two," Tempel growled. *"I'm fifty yards to your right, Lev. Fifteen seconds to punch through the surface and—"*

"Hold, Tempel," Levin said, lethal intent in his undertone.

The bastard. The uppity fucking *bastard*. Who in the hell did Biscayne think he was?

Levin's nostrils flared as he wrestled with his temper. Ice shards grew from the centers of his palms. Turning his hands, he hid his weapons in the web of his fingers. He shut down the squall next, wiping out the snowstorm gathering behind him, refusing to broadcast his intent...and the threat of imminent attack.

Henry should know better than to provoke a Dragonkind warrior—to demand that mated males return what no longer belonged to him. It was rude by every

Magickind standard. None too bright, either, given the ruthlessness of the Scottish pack.

"*End him,*" Rannock said, his need to protect Cate screaming through the connection. "*Cate never sees that bastard again. Ever. I donnae care if the feud with the Danish pack lasts a century.*"

"*Calm down, Ran,*" Levin said, knowing Vyroth felt the same way about Nicole. No way would either of his brothers allow their mates anywhere near Biscayne. Not after the abuse both had suffered at the hands of their sire. *"I've got him."*

Rannock blew past the one-mile marker.

Triple-bladed claws, followed by Tempel's talons, sliced through the turf like shark fins through water. Less than thirty feet behind Henry.

"Shell," Levin said, rotating the ice daggers in his hands.

Hearing the warning in his voice, the werewolf swallowed, then whispered a series of numbers. Remorse filled his dark eyes. "Levin...Lev...I sent her there. She needed to see, to quit poking around. Too obvious. Too dangerous, so I—"

Henry flexed his hand. Sharp nails punctured the wolf's skin. Pinpricks of blood appeared, then rolled, pooling in the hollow of Shell's clavicle as the vampire dragged him back into the shadows.

Shell rattled off the numbers again. "I promised, Levin, so promise me you'll go. It's not safe. It's not—"

"Shut up." Biscayne increased the pressure of his grip.

Lifeblood flowing, Shell gurgled.

Gaze burning into his, Levin repeated the numbers.

The wolf nodded, stoic resolve his eyes. A second later, he grabbed Henry's wrist. The vampire cursed as Shell drove sharp nails into his jugular. With a howl, he yanked, tearing his own throat wide open. Blood splattered across the ground, painting a tombstone red.

"Fuck," Biscayne said, jerking his arm back.

The werewolf hit the ground, heart still pumping, blood leaking into the dirt.

With a roar, Levin lunged toward the vampire. Eyes wide with shock, Biscayne cursed and scrambled backward. Tempel exploded from the ground in dragon form. Rock and dirt blew sky high as Levin flicked his wrists. Ice daggers flew. Sharp edges gleaming in the lowlight, his blades rotated end over end, whistling toward his target.

The vampire dove, tumbling into a sideways somersault.

Spiked tail flying, massive paws planted, Tempel tucked his wings and bared his fangs.

Running full tilt, Biscayne shifted course to avoid him. Legs churning, arms pinwheeling, he leapt over a low hedge. Levin went after him, unleashing more of his arsenal. Sharp shards of ice peppered the ground like bullets. The vampire veered right. Levin chased him down the path cutting between crypts, bombarding the arsehole with live ammo, tearing up the ground, toppling tombstones.

Biscayne darted into a small opening.

Gritting his teeth, Levin shoved his much larger frame between stone monoliths. He pushed himself harder, lengthened his stride, but...bloody hell. The bastard was fast. Slipping through thick hedges and over crumbling walls, outpacing Levin one stride at a time. He needed to shift into dragon form, but without time and more space, he'd end up losing Biscayne in the thicket, then eventually in city streets.

Lungs burning, feet churning, Levin slid around a corner. A blurry shadow moved beneath the trees up ahead. He threw another dagger sidearm. A thunk. A grunt of pain and the scuffling sound of stumbling.

The scent of vampire blood splashed into the air.

Levin snarled in triumph. Finally, a direct hit—one

he saw as the glamour shield around Biscayne wavered, allowing him to perceive the male…along with the blade sticking out of the back of the bastard's thigh.

He launched another, but pulled the throw, sending the weapon wide of its mark, slicing the outside of Biscayne's other leg. He needed Biscayne alive long enough to—

Pop!

Pop, pop…pop!

Magic that tasted toxic blasted up the alleyway. Howling wind flattened vegetation. Green vines turned black, dying as bright light flashed against stone, and Henry Biscayne disappeared into thin air.

3

Her ruined hand ached like the devil on damp days.

Though that wasn't saying much.

Priya Burman's once broken, badly healed knuckles hurt like hell at night too. All the time, actually. Tonight wasn't an exception. With rain falling hard on the road in front of her and the heater in her truck on the verge of quitting, everything hurt. Her body. Her hand. Her heart. But mostly her mind after she'd watched the video sent by an anonymous source she trusted but had never met.

Taking a cleansing breath, she pushed the awful images from her mind and kept her eyes on the road. The sight didn't bring her joy. Pouring rain. Desolate landscape shrouded in darkness. The headlights of her 1957 Land Rover barely pushing through the gloom, illuminating little more than five feet on the narrow road ahead of her.

No lights in the distance for her to go by. No houses or crofts fenced in behind low stone walls. Nothing but bleak, disjointed fields and dangerous curves snaking into the middle of nowhere.

She huffed into the silence floating like a rotten smell inside her truck. The heater ticked, fighting a losing battle against the chill as oversized tires slammed into a pothole and bounced out again. Her ass skipped off the seat and resettled against worn leather. Gritting her teeth, Priya swung around a tight S-curve.

She downshifted. The engine rumbled. Her truck swayed, hydroplaning across pitted asphalt.

The bump and grind felt like a warning.

Another in a long line of them since she'd packed an overnight bag and driven out of London. She'd crossed the border into Scotland hours ago, all the while wondering what in the hell had possessed her.

The thrill of the chase, maybe. The need to dig up details and expose criminals, for sure. It was a good cause, a story worth telling, but driving into the High-lands—alone, at night—qualified as crazy, even for her.

"Motherfucking madness," she muttered, swerving around a tree branch lying in the road.

The Rover rocked on its tires. The rain pelted the hood, slamming against steel, making it hard to see through the murk. Typical Highland weather. She was beginning to think her source might be a wingnut who came across as sane over the phone. The directions he'd provided didn't say much for him. Google Maps said even less. The stupid thing had been recalibrating for the last fifteen minutes.

She ran over another pothole.

The jolt jittered through her. Unease came calling. She wasn't sure, but...

She should be driving into town by now. Or at least seeing lights in the distance.

Peering out the fogged-up windshield, Priya frowned. Maybe she'd missed a turn. Maybe the entire night was a bust. And maybe, just maybe, her source had lied.

The realization made her want to turn around.

The file full of information Shell had promised made her keep driving. Just a few more miles. If she didn't locate the town soon, she'd find a safe spot to turn around and—

Her tires slammed into an even bigger pothole.

She cursed as heavy shocks rebounded. A loud bang reverberated. The cab rocked, tilting her dangerously to one side. The low stone wall on her left grazed the side of the steel bumper. Her heart in her throat, she double-clutched and downshifted, yanking her tank of an SUV back onto the road.

Sharp pain clawed over the back of her injured hand.

"Yeah," she said, jamming her knee against the underside of the wheel to help her steer. "One hundred percent. I'm absolutely out of my mind."

Pavement turned to dirt road. Two lanes narrowed into one. She checked the paper map propped up on the steering column. Her cell phone re-acquired a signal. The screen flashed as the map app came back on line and—

Her phone rang.

Her gaze flew to the Samsung sitting in a holder stuck to the dash. Relief spiraled through her. Well, at least she had that going for her.

She hadn't thought to check before leaving, but turned out, cell reception in the middle of nowhere was a bit of a crapshoot. Also a much-needed service while meeting an anonymous source just in case he ended up being a serial killer.

Not that calling the police would help if that turned out to be true. It wasn't as though the calvary would reach her way out here.

The phone kept ringing.

Seeing the name flashing on screen, Priya wanted to ignore the call. As a matter of course, avoiding her mother always worked best. Problem was…

Saanvi Burman rarely, if ever, took no for an answer.

It didn't matter that her mother now lived in a different country. Thousands of miles (along with the span of oceans) meant nothing to a woman on a mission. The cost of calling from Mumbai meant even less. The second Priya sent her to voicemail, her mother would hang up and call again until Priya got with her mother's program and answered the phone.

Mentally preparing herself, she tapped the green button. "Hi, Mum."

"Priya, my darling. I have the most delightful news."

"I can't talk right now." Pressing on the brakes, she rolled a stop and put the Rover in neutral. "I'm in the truck. It's raining. I'll call you back when I'm—"

"I found a matchmaker."

She blinked. "A what?"

"A matchmaker, darling. I've been doing some thinking."

"Please, God, no."

Her mother carried on, ignoring her, per usual. "After the catastrophe with Franklin… Not that I blame him, poor boy—"

"Poor boy?" Priya's eyes narrowed. Unbelievable. Totally twisted, and yet somehow typical. Her mother had always approved of her ex-fiancé. Not that Franklin had been a good guy, just a convenient one for her mother to lord over her friends during afternoon tea. "You can't be serious, Mum."

"Really, Priya." A rustle of fabric. The sound of a wooden spoon tapping against metal. Saanvi cleared her throat. "You could be a bit more understanding."

Her right eye started to twitch. "Understanding?"

"You know it couldn't have been easy for him… seeing you like that. Honestly, Priya, what did you expect him to do?"

"Stick by me, maybe? Wait until I got out of the hospital before breaking our engagement, at the very least?"

"You were a frightful sight, darling. No one would have expected him to—"

"Bullshit. He's a coward. A pretentious, shallow little prig."

"Priya, language!" her mother barked, voice crackling through the line. "I know it is still painful, but that is no excuse for vulgarity."

Her hand flexed on the steering wheel. She wanted to tell her mother to screw off and never call back. Good manners, ones ingrained in her from birth, stopped her. Priya sighed, knowing she should say to hell with politeness given the way her mother treated her—like a prize cow at auction—but arguing would only buy her more of Mother's time and attention.

"Can we talk later, Mum? I'm in the middle of—"

"Time moves on," Saanvi said. "And now, so must you. You are not getting any younger, Priya, and Abha informs me—"

"Who?"

"The matchmaker. Best in all of India. And let me tell you, it wasn't easy convincing her to take you on, but I managed to charm her. She's agreed—"

"God help me."

"—even in light of your *shortcomings*," her mother said, using the least offensive word to describe her scars. The marks Saanvi considered imperfections, the attack and the trauma somehow making Priya unsuitable, less than, a woman to pity instead of support. One of marriageable age that no man would want without the right incentive. "She says finding you a match will be difficult, but not impossible. She's already given me three candidates. Men from good families of sufficient status, wealth, and—"

"I'm not getting married."

"Every girl wants a husband, Priya."

"Not me."

"Don't be ungrateful."

"Papa wouldn't want this for me, and worse, you know it."

"Your father was a dreamer, Priya. He's gone, God rest his soul, buried in English soil, and you will not embarrass me in this way. You will speak with Abha. You will choose from the list of men she finds for you. Moving to India will be a blessing, darling. You'll see. You can stop chasing your silly stories. You'll have a husband and children to care for. You'll be—"

"Goodbye, Mum."

"Priya—"

Tapping the screen, she ended the call. Then she blocked all her mother's numbers. It wouldn't help. Saanvi would find another way to contact her. A burner phone, maybe. Enlisting a neighbor's help, perhaps. Sending a co-conspirator who still lived in the U.K. to her flat in London, always a possibility.

Staring at the crest on the steering wheel, Priya took a deep breath, then another, listening to the wipers creak. *Control.* She needed to control her temper. Right now, before she let anger loose and did something stupid—like grab her phone and chuck it out the window. Or find an airport and buy a ticket to Mumbai with the sole purpose of murdering her mother.

Her father wouldn't have blamed her. She knew, even in death, he understood the struggle was real, so…

"Arranged marriage, my ass," she said, scowling out into the rain.

No way that was happening, if for no other reason than her father would roll over in his grave. The man had been a saint. Putting up with his wife's antiquated ideas, standing strong for his daughter.

Priya closed her eyes.

God, how she missed him. His smile. His laughter. His voice, so soft and gentle. He'd had a way with a kind word, and a shrewdness unmatched by anyone she knew. Instead of stifling her creativity, Papa had encouraged her, giving her complicated puzzles to solve and codes to break, fostering her love of true crime stories, refusing to allow her to be shamed and manipulated by her mother.

He'd been proud of her—so very proud. Which meant she couldn't be anything less than proud of herself. For holding the line. For doing what she loved. For digging deep and helping those unable to help themselves, so…

Time to get back on track.

Shifting into first gear, she urged the Rover forward. The GPS began talking to her. She turned onto what amounted to a cattle trail, and once again questioned her sanity, along with her source's motives.

Shell seemed like a solid guy. Smart, funny, if somewhat left of center. But he hadn't been wrong yet, and he'd been feeding her information for months. First, to help her solve a cold case the Metropolitan Police had given up on years ago. Then to feed her information about a corrupt politician and the cohort of corporate thugs he used to stay in power. Now to assist her in exposing an abusive cult masquerading as a wellness community in the Scottish Highlands.

He was a valuable source.

He was also a major pain in the ass. One who, until twenty-four hours ago, had insisted on remaining anonymous. But given the stakes, and the monster story she was chasing, she needed to be sure—of him, of herself, and the facts. No stone could be left unturned. Which meant Shell's need for anonymity no longer worked for her. She needed to meet with him.

It had taken time, but after months spent building trust, she'd convinced him to come in from the cold. Or step out of the dark. Whatever. The expression didn't matter. All that mattered was he had the information she needed—the file that laid out a paper trail so crooked, so undeniable, it would tear the case wide open.

Landing the story would prove everyone around her wrong. She wasn't washed up. Despite her colossal screw-up, being attacked didn't mean she couldn't do her job. She wasn't flawed. She wasn't ruined. She was smart, strong, and independent. Not incompetent, no matter what everyone else thought.

One night two years ago, a single miscalculation, culminating in a month-long hospital stay, and the trust she built over the years had been lost. Gone in an instant.

No one believed in her anymore. The paper wanted her to stay behind the microphone, churning out episodes of *Salt in the Wound*, the true crime podcast she'd started after the attack. It was a good gig. She liked it. The money she made doing it kept her afloat, but talking about cold cases, retelling old stories on a podcast, wasn't all she could do. Wasn't all she was *meant* to do.

She was a journalist. A damned good one, but...

Even her editor at the *Guardian* wanted her to play it safe. He urged her to stay on the sidelines and let others lead. To stop investigating the hard cases and go after fluffier ones. At first, she'd listened, shying away from meeting sources for fear of being attacked again. Two years of being held back and cooped up. Twenty-four months of being afraid, of doing what everyone else wanted, but now...

It was time.

What she needed was a break, a serious story no one would be able to ignore. A way to make her former colleagues respect her again. Which meant she couldn't turn back now.

Shell held the final pieces of the puzzle. She needed the file.

Though Thomas (editor in chief at the *Guardian*)

would ask hard questions when she showed up in his office with the evidence in hand. The good, bad, and ugly would come out then. He'd lose his mind when she told him she'd met her source alone—on a desolate stretch of a terribly kept road deep in the Scottish Highlands, of all places.

He'd yell.

She'd pretend to listen.

In the end, the story would get published and the world would be better for it. The police would get involved. People would be saved and justice served.

Idealistic, maybe, but Priya believed it. The rabbit holes she traveled down unearthed skeletons and dug up truths, leveling lopsided playing fields when it came to righting wrongs in the world. The reporter in her wanted to shine a light into those dark places. The woman in her, however, understood the danger.

She'd learned firsthand the hard way.

Monsters lived in the shadows, on the fringes of society, dragging innocent people into places they didn't belong. Some, like her, ended up hurt. Others, not as lucky, ended up dead.

Glancing down at her hand, she forced her crooked fingers to bend. Shards of bone ground together. Pain carved a sharp path up her forearm.

Keeping her foot on the gas pedal, she cracked open the small cooler sitting on the passenger seat. Curls of fog whispered over the raised scars on her skin. Watching the Rover's headlights eat through the gloom, she leaned sideways, plunging her hand into icy water.

Immediate relief.

With a sigh, she made figure eights with her hand. Ice cubes knocked against her wrist. Taut muscles unlocked. Tension downgraded, sharpening her focus as she fished for the cast resting at the bottom. Molded plastic on the outside, gel on the inside, a special blend trapped inside soft packs that stayed cold for hours against her skin.

Gaze on the road, she pulled the cast from the water. Droplets fell across her the tops of her thighs. She tore open thick Velcro, then slipped her hand inside and tightened the straps, setting the cast in place. Like magic, ice-cold gel went to work. Minutes ticked past. The pain moved from a brutal throb to an annoying blip.

Traditional doctors couldn't explain it. Neither could her naturopath. And her wellness coach? Forget about it. She'd met with dozens of experts. Everyone was stumped, throwing out theories, making crap up, marveling she never got frostbite. But after having most of the bones in her hand broken, Priya welcomed respite in whatever form it arrived.

Ice baths. Snowbanks. Icicles pulled from the freezer. The source of cold didn't matter, just as long as her hand remained numb and her mind stayed sharp.

The engine rumbled as she drove up a steep rise.

At the top, the rain dried up, moving from downpour to light sprinkle. Gloomy skies lightened. The clouds cleared. Clusters of stars winked down from the night sky. A weird buzz rolled through the truck, raising the fine hairs at the back of her neck, and—

Color undulated across the clearing. A rainbow rose above wet grass, arching up to touch the sky. The colorful wash landed on the other side of the dell and began to glow, the array of color so startling she almost missed seeing the lone tree standing on the fair side of the dell.

The great oak sat beside a croft with a thatch roof.

The spot Shell had asked her to meet him.

Bumping up the lane over uneven ground, Priya drove toward house. The rainbow shimmered above her, painting the small valley, dancing across horseshoe-shaped cliffs rising beyond the croft.

With a flick, she turned off the wipers. Silence fell inside the cab as her gaze roamed. Dark night and brilliant colors. The dell felt mystical, as though it had been pulled from another time and place. As though it belonged anywhere but here, and she was trespassing, standing in a place people didn't belong, witnessing something nature wanted to keep to herself.

A ridiculous thought, but...

What a sight.

She'd heard the old wives' tales, stories told in hushed tones about vibrant fairy glens in Scottish fables. Sane people didn't believe them, but as she drove toward the tree, Priya smiled, wanting, for the first time in her life, to believe in magic. In the idea that some things couldn't, and never would be, explained. That beauty didn't always need to be seen in order to exist.

Dragging her gaze from the rainbow, she scanned the front of the croft. No vehicle parked off to the side. No lights on inside. No footprints in the wet grass or tire tracks in the lane ahead of her. Where the hell was he? Shell had told her he'd be waiting, assuring her he'd bring what he promised, hand over the file, and—

Movement flashed in her periphery.

Her head snapped toward the driver's-side window.

She caught sight of something. Time slowed down without stopping. Her mind took a snapshot, framing a hulking figure covered in dark, shaggy fur. Huge paws tipped by long, bladed claws. Sharp fangs in an open mouth full of jagged teeth, moving so fast its body blurred as it streaked toward her.

Bright yellow eyes with vertical pupils met hers through the glass.

It snarled.

She screamed, scrambling to put the Rover in reverse.

Running full tilt, the beast rammed the side of her SUV. Steel crumpled. Her door bowed inward. Glass shattered, throwing shards across the cab as, engine screaming, the truck left the ground, tumbling into the air.

Her seatbelt yanked her back into the seat.

Air exploded from her lungs.

With an inhuman howl, the monster attacked again. And again, spinning the vehicle like a top, tossing her around like a rag doll inside the cab.

4

The numbers were written in blood. Scratched into the dirt by broken fingernails.

Gaze on the messy scrawl, Levin hit his haunches next to Shell's body. His temper spiked. Magic hissed through his veins. Ice crystals exploded into flurries as his bare feet churned in the loose soil south of the blood pool.

Fuck. It was everywhere—seeping into the ground, splashed over tombstone faces, running in rivulets down the front of the werewolf's chest. Planting his forearms on his widespread thighs, Levin looked up to meet dead eyes. Dark as pitch, wide open, full of shock, staring up into gentle snowfall. Snowflakes landed on him, then melted, leaving tiny droplets on the wolf's face.

Levin clenched his teeth.

Punk-ass motherfucker. What in the hell had Shell been thinking? Had he waited, Levin would've figured out a way to get him out safely. Maybe not in one piece, but alive while he and his packmates locked down Biscayne.

Instead, Shell had jumped the gun, tearing his own throat out, protecting Levin by giving the only thing he truly owned—his life. Such a high cost. So much trauma, and for what? To ensure Levin paid attention to a bunch of numbers?

His gaze tracked to the message scratched in the dirt.

Longitude followed by latitude. He made a few quick calculations. His eyes narrowed as he opened his senses. His dragon half went to work, dropping a magical net over the location and—

His sonar pinged.

Levin hummed. X marked the spot, in the middle of nowhere west of Aberdeen, buried deep inside the Grampian Mountains. Shell's last-ditch effort at redemption, though...

Levin didn't yet know what it meant. Or why the wolf expected him to fly all the way out there.

Something about a *she*.

Something about it not being safe.

A mystery. The kind Shell knew he'd never be able to resist.

In life, the wolf had been a pain in the arse. He was proving to be the same in death, but that didn't mean Levin wasn't interested. His history with the werewolf provided context. The entire reason he'd made the trip to Nellfield Cemetery was knowing the werewolf would point him in the right direction, providing answers to some major questions. Ones Levin needed to eliminate the enemy and protect his pack.

Myriad possible scenarios came to mind. Only two held enough power to hold his attention. Possibility number one—the location of the Danes' primary lair. Possibility number two—the whereabouts of the rogue Druids who wanted Ferguson, newly anointed innkeeper of The White Hare, dead.

Levin hoped for the first. He wanted to make Grizgunn, commander of the Danes, bleed. Tear the bastard limb from limb for invading his territory and tormenting those under his pack's protection. Humans, Magickind—it didn't matter to Grizgunn whom he hurt. The more carnage left in his wake, the better the male liked it. So information about where the bastard laid his head each day topped the list of things Levin wanted to know.

Logic, however, suggested Shell's coordinates pointed to something else. Another mess, one in a long line of them with Shell. A situation Levin knew he needed to be clean up, given the promise Shell forced him to make—and the warning that *she* wasn't safe.

Closing his eyes, he pressed his chin to his chest. Taut muscles stretched. Pain nipped along his spine. He assessed the problem. A series of numbers. Not much else to go on…other than *she*. Nameless. Faceless. A female in trouble, put in there by a werewolf who couldn't be trusted to look out for himself, much less anyone else. Though, in the end, Shell had reached for redemption, deciding to put someone other than himself first for a change.

Cracking his neck, Levin listened to the snap and replayed the scene, letting it roll like a movie in his mind's eye. The wolf's desperation had been real, his panic full-blown. The idiot had sent someone somewhere into something dangerous. Into a place so wild, so savage, most Magickind avoided it, refusing to tempt fate and anger the Goddess. No one really knew what lay at the heart of the Grampian Mountains. Not even Levin. He'd never cared enough to wonder, never mind explore what might call the—

"Did you see that?" The snick of claws sounded on flagstone. A metallic tang drifted across the clearing. Scales rattled as Rannock shifted, moving from dragon to human form. "Biscayne disappeared into thin air."

"I saw," Levin murmured, keeping his eyes on Shell.

Rannock's boots came into view. His friend stopped beside the blood pool. "You get a sense of it, Lev? Close enough tae clock it?"

"Cloaking spell?" Green scales covered in dirt, Tempel leapt over a stone archway. His spiked tail whipped, slashing through a hedge. Branches tumbled end over end, bouncing off the hard shell of his interlocking dragon skin. "Wormhole?"

"Dematerialization," Levin said, pushing to his feet. "Fae magic."

Rannock grunted. "Ye're shitting me."

Tilting his head back, Levin looked at his friend. "Nay."

"You sure?" Triple-bladed claws curled around a stone angel, Tempel settled into a crouch on top of a high crypt. "You've seen it used before?"

Levin shook his head. "Read about it. There's a section in the lair library about the Ancient Tribes. Thick volumes full of information on the Fae."

Tempel frowned. "Thought they were extinct."

"Apparently not," Levin said, coming to a conclusion, and not liking it. "Biscayne's got tribal blood in him."

"Shite," Rannock growled. "I'm going tae enjoy killing the bastard."

His lips twitched. "Gotta find him first, Ran."

"At the meet," Tempel said. "When he shows up at The White Hare."

"Nay." Shaking his head, Levin pieced together the facts. "We canna kill Biscayne on the grounds. There are rules all Magickind must abide by inside the Parkland."

"Fuck the rules." Bronze gaze sparking, wearing fury like cologne, Rannock cracked his knuckles. "He's after my mate."

"You wanna butt heads with Fergie?"

Alarm took a trip across Rannock's face. "No way. She'll—"

"Tear you a new asshole before she turns you to ash," Tempel said from his perch.

An understatement.

A magic wielder of immense power, the innkeeper ruled with a big heart and an iron fist. She kept tabs on her guests and got creative when meting out punishments to those stupid enough to step out of line. Fergie never allowed the rules to be broken. The most important one sat at the very top of the list—no killing on hotel grounds. A code of conduct every conclave of Magickind obeyed inside 173 hectares of the most pristine woodland in all of Scotland.

The second a guest took another's life inside her domain, the Parkland reacted, and Ferguson made her presence known. She didn't hesitate. She ended the perpetrator's life. An eye for an eye. A system that worked well when dealing with the most vicious species alive.

"Biscayne doesnae get near Cate, Lev," Rannock said, voice soft, violence underpinning each syllable. "Nowhere near her, you hear?"

"I hear, and he willnae, brother," he murmured. "We'll figure out a way to get Biscayne off the grounds. The second he crosses out of Fergie's territory, he's fair game."

Rannock grunted.

Tempel pointed a talon at the ground. "What's that?"

"Numbers." Sidestepping him, Rannock crouched, eyes pinned to the message now saturated in blood. "A location."

Levin nodded. "Aye."

"To where?" Tempel asked.

"The Grampians," Levin said, curiosity now an itch he wanted to scratch.

Tempel raised a scaly brow. "We going?"

"Bloody werewolf," Rannock said. "Crazy as fuck."

"Mayhap, but..." Levin pushed to his feet. "We're going."

"Got better things tae do, mon," Rannock said. "Wanna go home. Check on Cate."

"We check this out first." Staring at the dead wolf, Levin murmured his wishes. Ice crackled around the werewolf, freezing him into a solid block. He flicked his fingers. Arctic cold swirled in, causing Shell's body to hover above the ground. With a mental command, he opened the door to the crypt, pushing his informant inside, then slammed it closed behind him. "I wanna know what's out there. Why Shell made me promise."

A muscle twitching in his jaw, Rannock flexed his hands. "My mate—"

"Give it a break, Ran." Erasing all traces of violence, Levin finished cleaning up. Magic swirled over the ground. Spilled blood disappeared, the numbers Shell scratched into the dirt along with it. "Cate isnae expecting you home for hours. And honestly, she could do with a break from the likes of you."

Baring his fangs, Tempel laughed.

"Ye're just jealous." Mischief in his bronze eyes, Rannock smiled. "My mate loves me."

True.

Cate did love his friend. Deeply. Completely. She showed Rannock how much he meant to her every day.

Levin sighed as another truth hit him.

Rannock had been teasing, but Levin *was* jealous. Green with fucking envy.

Each time he dreamed. Every time she came to him in his sleep, the craving for her worsened, and his discontentment grew. Levin loved the warriors he fought alongside each night, but sometimes, it was hard watching his brothers with their chosen females. He spent a lot of time studying them, looking for the magic, trying to understand each pairing—the deep love, the absolute acceptance, the unshakable commitment each of his packmates enjoyed with the female made and meant for him.

Energy-fuse, such an intense connection.

The magical bond between mates aligned hearts and minds, stitching souls together. A cosmic weave so powerful, so rare, Dragonkind males searched for it their entire lives, longing for the female who vibrated at the same energetic frequency. Most never managed to find her. A curse handed down as punishment by the Goddess of All Things, but curiously, one that hadn't yet touched the Scottish pack. Six of the eight had been fortunate enough to not only find, but claim their mates.

Statistics suggested his brothers-in-arms had defied the odds.

Levin wanted to believe it was something else. The work of a divine hand, mayhap. Hope in the idea the Goddess favored his pack, blessing them with what every Dragonkind male wanted—a female to call his own. One he could love, care for, and sire bairns with without causing her death. So…

The extreme yearning was real. A constant for him inside a lair full of couples. Which explained his obsession with the female haunting his dreams.

He wanted what his packmates had—an unbreakable connection with the one made for him. Someone to fly home to at the end of each night. Someone to hold while he slept. Someone to cherish and spoil while awake. And no matter how absurd it sounded, Levin recognized his dream lass. He'd never met her, didn't know her name or where she lived, but his dragon half acknowledged her the instant he saw her.

She belonged to him.

He belonged to her. Wholly. Without reasoning why or needing to understand.

Logic didn't factor. She wasn't a figment of his

imagination. She was real, somewhere out in the world, living her life without him. Not knowing where to find her was killing him, slowly, little by little each day. Having her face inked into his arm helped soothe the yearning, but that didn't mean he couldn't wait for morning to come. For the moment he crawled into bed and closed his eyes, hoping to see her. She never disappointed, coming to him as he dropped into sleep, walking to him across frozen tundra. Brown skin glowing with vitality. Dark eyes shining with secrets. Long hair flowing in dark waves behind her.

Gorgeous. Fucking spectacular, and—

"Loves you, my ass. You're full of shit, Ran," Tempel said, tone teasing, aiming to start a fight. "Didn't Cate threaten to gut you three hours ago?"

"Foreplay, mon." True to his Metallic roots, embracing crazy in all forms, Rannock grinned. "It's a beautiful thing."

Tempel laughed.

"No more fucking around," Levin said, relegating his dream lass to the back of his mind. Sunrise would come soon enough. In sleep, the world would tilt back in his favor, allowing him to experience her in living color again. "Let's go."

Glowing green eyes met his. "Backup?"

Glancing up at the sky, Levin nodded. "Make the call, T. Everyone in the air. All claws on deck."

Leaving Rannock to follow, he pivoted and turned up the trail. He strode past the spot Biscayne disappeared, nothing but the mission on his mind. Gravel crunched under his bare feet, then gave way to a grassy knoll. Stepping onto the turf, he leapt from the ground onto the statue of a horse, hooves rearing, human rider tilted backward, and launched himself skyward.

He shifted into dragon form mid-jump.

His body lengthened as his bones cracked. Scales the color of multi-hued icebergs fell like dominos. His hands and feet transformed into huge paws tipped by lethal midnight-blue claws. Opening his wings, he rocketed into open skies. Contrails streaming from his wingtips, he blasted out of Aberdeen. City lights dimmed, becoming pinpoint flashes beneath him. A low growl sounded as Rannock and Tempel joined him in flight, one to his left, the other to his right.

Static blew into his head. A connection into mind-speak opened.

Tempel's voice tapped on his frontal lobe. *"Boys are on the way. Time to intercept—ten minutes."*

Levin tipped his chin. *"Good. Got a feeling we're gonna need the firepower."*

"Bloody werewolf," Rannock murmured, throwing him a baleful look. *"Fly all the way out there, we better find a fight."*

Goddess willing.

After weeks of hunting Grizgunn without success, frustration was turning into fury. Soon, the collective rage inside the Scottish lair would boil over, so...aye. Levin needed what Rannock wanted—a claw-grinding, scale-scorching, fang-baring fight. He wasn't picky. He'd accept it in whatever form it took, just as long it arrived.

Rannock grumbled something nasty under his breath.

Gaze on distant mountain peaks, Levin ignored his friend and plugged the coordinates into his internal GPS. A radar screen flared in his mind's eye. Twisting the powerful magic he controlled, Levin upped the voltage, then dropped an invisible net over rough terrain. The grid expanded, rushing out in front of him, blanketing the landscape, providing him with more information.

Clear skies. No Danes in the vicinity. Thunder rumbling in the distance.

Wind whistling over his horns, Levin flew toward

the eye of the storm, tracking the longs and lats, heading toward the pin drop on his mental map. A place instinct warned him would do one of two things —provide the answers he needed to hunt and kill the enemy, or add more problems to the pile, the kind of trouble none of them needed right now.

5

The seatbelt wrenched tight as the Rover left its tires, spinning into a sideways tumble.

Trapped inside the truck, Priya sucked in a choked breath. The crunch of buckling metal rang in her ears. Glass shattered. A strange clicking noise sounded. Compressing herself into as small a ball as she could, she closed her eyes and hung on tight, waiting for the SUV to stop rolling.

The revolving ride slowed.

The Rover teetered and, in what felt like slow motion, rolled onto its roof.

Priya heard the engine tick. She felt the tightness of the belt locking her in, holding her immobile, strangling her in her seat. She drew in another raspy breath. When that didn't work, she concentrated on unlocking her lungs. Little by little, air returned. Her chest expanded and the pain came, spiking through her collarbone, spiraling over her shoulder and—

A metallic taste flooded her mouth.

Swallowing the awful tang, she opened her eyes and, fighting seized muscles, raised her hand. The cast she wore brushed her chin. Her crooked fingers touched her lip and came away covered in red. She stared at it a moment before comprehension dawned.

Blood in her mouth, running down her chin, a sharp sting along in her jaw. She ran her tongue along the raw patch where her teeth had gouged the inside of her mouth.

Long gash. An open wound. But unlike the old ones, the cut was hidden from view.

Staring unseeing out the cracked windshield, she took a moment to realize she was hanging upside down. Hair dangling, body suspended, pinned in place by a thick vinyl strap manufactured in the 1950s. A miracle the thing had held.

The vintage truck might be tough, but that didn't mean the stuff inside it wasn't old and worn, tired to the point it was sometimes faulty.

Heart hammering, ears still ringing, she turned her head to look out the driver's-side window. Shattered. Nothing but jagged shards of glass sticking out of a bent doorframe.

Her brows contracted. What the hell happened? One minute she'd been driving along, minding her own business. The next, she'd been airborne, thrown, flipped by—

The strange clicking came again.

From somewhere outside the SUV.

A suctioning, squishy noise drifted into the cab. Sounded like someone approaching from across the field. A farmer, maybe. Someone who lived in the area, coming to help get her out of the truck.

Priya opened her mouth to call out.

Two huge hooves landed on the ground beside the passenger side door. Self-preservation tried to tell her it was a horse. Her mind kicked over, screaming that it wasn't. Horses didn't have hooves like that—spilt-toed, with lethal-looking sawtooth blades rimming the edges.

Frozen in her seat, hanging upside down, barely breathing, Priya watched as the thing standing outside nudged the Rover. Steel groaned as the roof slid across muddy ground. The beast came down on all fours. Bladed hooves for back feet, but not on its forelegs. Long, thin, hooked claws tipped front paws that looked like human hands. And on its body? Shaggy brown fur the color of a grizzly bear's. Standing like a gorilla, the beast folded thick fingers under and leaned forward, resting the weight of its upper body on its knuckles.

What little breath she had left in a hurry, compressing her chest.

Oh no.

Shitty-shit-shit!

More clicking and—

Another pair of bladed hooves landed in front of the hood. A third sloshed through the mud next to her on the driver's side.

Her lip quivered as fear ravaged good sense. Adrenaline burned through her veins. Her heart, already pounding, started hammering the inside of her breastbone. Terror blurring her ability to think, she reached for buckle on her seat. Hand hovering over the button, she watched the hooves move around the Rover. Panic urged her to press down, hope the lock wasn't jammed after her violent tumble and run. Prudence arrived in the nick of time, warning her to do the opposite.

Blood pounding in her temples, Priya tucked her hands against her chest, subduing the natural inclination to free herself. She couldn't see much, but everything about the beasts screamed *predator*. The kind that loved to give chase…and eat whatever it caught. The second she left the Rover, the things would do what nature intended—hunt and kill. So…

Running wouldn't save her. Staying silent and still, however, just might.

Hands trembling, Priya swallowed past the lump in her throat and, ticking off boxes inside her head, forced herself to come up with a plan. Step one—control her breathing. Step two—steady her heartbeat. Step three—think instead of panic. The creatures hadn't found her yet. Maybe, with the scent of mud and motor oil in the air, they couldn't smell her. Maybe immense strength and violent instincts compensated for blunted senses. She didn't know, but the second she moved, the beasts circling her would figure it out.

Find her.

Drag her from the truck.

Then eat her alive.

Taking a shallow breath, she tried to problem-solve, but...God help her. Her mind kept returning to the nightmare. Worse than her worst fear come to life. It was, after all, difficult to imagine being afraid of something she hadn't known existed until now.

The troop of big, dark, and scary continued searching, making sweeping turns around her truck. One by one, others joined the trio. She counted six...no, seven...of the things now. All making the strange clicking sounds, talking to one another, searching, circling, pushing against steel side panels, sending the Rover into a slow, wobbly spin.

One rotation spun into another. And another, twirling her across open ground in a sick version of ballroom dancing.

Priya closed her eyes. Sooner or later, the beasts would work it out and know she was inside. Caged by metal, belted in, easy pickings for the weird mishmash of bear-gorilla creatures determined to sniff her out.

A bang sounded.

Metal groaned. The body of the Rover shuddered.

Long hair hanging above her head, Priya looked toward the floorboards. Hooves tapped across the undercarriage, driving the roof of her truck into the soft ground. The heavy steel frame buckled. Cables snapped. Fine fissures spread across the already cracked windshield as muddy water streamed in through the broken windows.

Wet touched the crown of her head, soaking her hair.

The radio hissed.

In a panic, she hit the off button.

The clicking intensified, and—

Sharp claws sliced through the undercarriage, and she got her first look good look at it. Flat face with blunt features. A piggish nose with two slits for nostrils. Winged, batlike ears on its head. Round eyes with yellow pupils met hers through the hole. The creature bared its razor-sharp teeth. Priya opened her mouth to scream. She didn't get the chance. Quicker than her, the monster sliced the floorboard, opening it like a tin can.

Leathery fingers curled inward.

Her seat jerked.

Bolts snapped, then she was being dragged, still belted in, out of her truck by the bottom of her seat with driver's door still attached. The one who held her jumped down. Hooves slammed into the ground. Mud splashed into her face as the creature swung her full circle, showing her off, giving her whiplash, making her vision blur as the surroundings whirled.

The troop howled in triumph.

Holding part of the Rover's frame aloft, the monster came to an abrupt stop. She swayed in her seat. Yellow eyes trained on her, bladed teeth bared, the beast raised its other hand.

Hooked claws slashed toward her.

Time slowed. Shock pummeled her as regret tunneled deep. Vibrant images lit up the screen inside her mind: Happy times with her father. Messy standoffs with her mother. Laughter and time spent with friends. The work and stories that fed her soul. She'd paid her dues, scraped and sacrificed, enduring more than any woman should be expected to, and…

God.

She wasn't supposed to die this way. Slowly. Horribly. Served up like a meal to creatures who shouldn't exist by a source she believed was trustworthy.

She still had things to do. So many stories left to tell and people to help. None of that mattered now. Not while she hung upside down, seconds away from being gutted by an animal that defied the laws of nature.

Long, sharp claws sliced toward her belly.

She wanted to be brave, to be stoic and silent, fearless in her final moments, but that didn't happen. Tears welled, coming fast, falling furious as the creature slashed through her jacket, and she screamed into the face of death.

6

On point, his brothers-in-arms flying in formation behind him, Levin rocketed out of the clouds into open skies. Magic whirled around him. Cold air collided with damp. Heavy mist washed into the mountainside, curled along his flank, slithering around the spikes riding his spine. Locked on to a distant target, he banked hard, zigzagging around jagged outcroppings, carving a path across the unforgiving mountain range.

Tilting his wings, he sliced around a steep cliff face. Wind hissed over his scales. His sonar pinged. The coordinates given to him by Shell throbbed against the inside of his skill as thunder rumbled and the sky opened up.

Sheets of rain started to fall.

The deluge coated him, turning to ice on contact as he exploded out of the mist like a bullet shot from a gun—with aim, intent, and the willingness to kill anyone in his path.

Nothing new there.

Each time he left the lair, every time he flew, high velocity and extreme aggression combined, melding until he became a stone-cold killing machine.

To be expected, given his subset of Dragonkind.

His beast was cold and cunning, full of ice, frost, and ill will. Emotion never factored, or pushed him off a target. He didn't give a shite what anyone thought of the chilly demeanor he wore like armor. He rode the edge wild, pushing the envelope, operating in areas no one else wanted to—the dark places, the ambiguous and gray...not caring whom he hurt most nights.

His brothers-in-arms loved him for it, embraced his viciousness, relying on the dragnet of information he pulled to the surface with methods most considered unethical. His edginess now, though, had nothing to do with his staying sharp during a covert operation.

There was nothing *covert* about what he planned to do.

The next ten minutes was about sound and fury. The more noise he made flying into the valley ahead, the better. Whoever lived there needed to know they'd fucked up...and now had company in the form of an entire Dragonkind contingent. A sight no one, no matter how powerful, wanted to see land in their backyard.

Rechecking the longs and lats, Levin narrowed his focus. Almost there. A few more minutes, and he'd hit the three-mile marker, and beyond that, the valley where he sensed enemy movement. The stench riding on the night breeze alerted him. The intense vibe in the air did the rest as his packmates played follow the leader, keeping pace behind him.

A rare occurrence.

Most nights, he flew out of the lair with just one wing-mate watching his six. Brutal to the point of self-destruction, Rannock had always been his first choice. Though, lately, Tempel had gotten in on the action, providing cover, listening and learning as Levin went about his business. Meeting current CIs, recruiting new ones, digging through the constant flow of information, pulling intel from human and Magickind sources alike. Which meant he rarely got to fly with the group anymore. To feel the collective power of his pack, or be awed by the males he called brothers.

A shame, really. The warriors at his back packed a serious punch. None of them had ever let him down. And no wonder, given each had been born to a high-energy female, ensuring the magic they wielded, along with the accompanying skill sets, topped the charts. Earth dragon. Fire dragon. Ice dragon. Venomous, Acid, or Metallic—the subset of Dragonkind didn't matter. Not when it came to the males he shared a lair with beneath The Dragon's Horn (the pub owned by the Scottish pack) in Aberdeen.

He and his brothers were heavyweights, the crème de la crème, in a world where Dragonkind ruled.

Enjoying the load of vicious at his back, Levin smiled. Snow swirled in his field of vision. He sucked the chill between his teeth, then went wings vertical, blasting between twin mountain peaks, his attention fixed on the beacon beating on his radar screen.

Steep decline on his right. High cliff on his left. With a quick twist, he flipped up and over the vertical face, then blasted down the other side. Stone cracked against stone. Snow and shale tumbled into an avalanche, ripping boulders from the mountainside.

The cascade jackhammered across the night sky. The cloaking spell around him shuddered. Violent sound rippled, streaming over peaks and valleys, slamming into the target zone.

Rannock huffed in amusement.

Flying off his wingtip, Tempel grinned.

"Well met, Lev," Cyprus said, laughter in his voice. *"Fair play—givin' 'em a warning. Though gotta say, mon, a surprise, since you've never felt the need tae play that way before."*

Levin grunted. *"I wanna a good fight, Cy, not a fast one. Thinking this'll make it more interesting."*

"Fuck," Tydrin murmured, orange flames licking over his dark purple scales. *"I hope so."*

"Goddess willing," Vyroth growled at the same time. *"I could use a good fight."*

"Donnae get yer hopes up, lads," Wallaig said, forever the voice of reason.

"Fuck you, auld mon." Throwing the pack's second-in-command a dirty look, Kruger lashed out with his tail. Emerald-green spikes clanged against Wallaig's blood-red scales. The male grunted. Kruger scowled. *"Donnae ruin my fun before it begins."*

Ignoring the byplay, Levin banked around a lop-sided tower sculpted by Mother Nature. The valley came into view. Two and a half miles out, less than three minutes to target. He bared his fangs. Frost gathering on the serrated tips, he upped his wing speed, then let more sound out of the bubble.

A cacophony of beating wings throbbed across high cliffs into the foothills.

He heard his brothers-in-arms chuckle.

Levin ignored that too.

Forewarning the troop of warnocks in the distance seemed like the best course of action. Also the optimal way to obtain his objective.

Cognitive abilities blunted by years of inbreeding, no one who knew anything about Magickind would call warnocks smart. That didn't mean, however, their hearing wasn't sharp. A loud noise would alert the troop's Alpha. The greater the threat, the faster she would round up the group and head for cover—back into the caves Levin guessed must be close, given warnocks never stayed aboveground long.

Druids who embraced the dark arts preferred it that way.

Spliced together by a master wizard centuries ago, warnocks acted like a strike force for Druid tribes gone rogue. After coming aboveground for a quick kill, troops retreated deep into the earth just as fast. Smart if deployed for righteous reasons. A useful tool in ancient times when protecting kin, hearth, and home from the enemy.

War between rival Druid tribes, however, had twisted original intent, transforming what amounted to pets into killing machines that attacked at will and without provocation. A dangerous play for dominance. A game ethical tribes refused to play, mostly by refusing to breed warnocks in the modern age.

Dark Druids, unfortunately, didn't abide by the peace treaties signed two hundred and fifty years ago. Those who lived outside the law, after all, were never any good at abiding by, or respecting it.

Which made a ton of sense, given what lay ahead.

Rogue tribes never hesitated to put warnocks to work. Which told Levin what he needed to know. And why the werewolf wanted him here. Shell had caught a putrid scent. Like the male always did, he'd nailed down the details, ensuring the intel was solid, then brought it to Levin and...

Ended up dead for his trouble.

So...

No need to speculate. The CI's message came through loud and clear.

The warnocks Levin scented belonged to the Druids his pack hunted. The clan who called itself Legion was cunning and shifty. Shadow dwellers who'd proven difficult to track. A newly acquired enemy of the Scottish pack, Legion took arseholery to new heights—attacking peaceful Druid tribes, leaving no one alive in their wake...attempting to murder Kruger's mate, the new innkeeper at The White Hare, with an eye to controlling the magical properties of Parkland.

A wild stab at accruing more power, a dangerous strategy deployed by arseholes punching above their weight class.

Diving over the last rise, Levin blasted toward the valley floor. He pinged his packmates. *"Thirty seconds tae target. Tempel, with me. The rest of you, break off, fan out, and set up. Clock anyone coming in or out."*

Bright orange wings spread wide, black and white scales flashing, Cyprus broke from formation first. *"Banking east."*

"On yer six," Tydrin said, following his commander.

Fire twisting off his horns like mini-tornados, Wallaig bared his fangs. *"I'll set up on the western range."*

"I'm with you," Kruger growled, contrails streaming off his wingtips.

Without saying a word, Rannock and Vyroth banked at the same time. Speed supersonic, the pair blasted across the night sky, one moving north, the other south.

"Lay it out, Lev." Flipping up and over, Tempel rolled in on his right side. *"What've we got?"*

"You donnae smell it?"

"Oh, I smell it," Tempel said, nose wrinkling. *"I just don't know what it is."*

"Warnocks."

Tempel threw him a questioning look. *"What the hell is that?"*

"You'll see," he murmured, fighting the need to gag. He couldn't help it. The stench of the creatures was potent, making his eyes water from half a mile away. *"Need you tae tag the first one you see with yer earth magic."*

"We tracking?"

"Aye. Underground warren. My guess, a series of interconnected caves. Gonna play follow the leader, see who the beasts return tae."

"Legion," his friend growled.

Levin nodded. *"Track, hunt, and kill."*

A nasty gleam in his eyes, Tempel smiled. *"Out-fucking-standing."*

Absolutely right.

The troop provided an excellent opportunity. A chance for him and his pack to eliminate one of the problems nipping at their heels. An outcome that would end up messy and lethal by the end of the night. At least for Legion.

"Rivers of blood," Levin said, violence in his undertone.

His wing-mate threw him a sidelong look. *"What?"*

"Little rivers of blood running down my claws."

"You visualizing?"

"Manifesting."

"You gonna leave any of the enemy for me?"

"Be quick, little brother. Be very, very quick if you want tae get yer claws bloody."

Tempel laughed.

Levin fined-tuned his sonar, then threaded the needle, slicing between a series of enormous stone towers. The magical barrier hanging over the valley vibrated. Color exploded in waves, arching from a clearing hemmed in by thick woods on one side and cliffs on the other.

Tempel flinched. *"Holy fuck."*

"Steady," Levin murmured, feeling the burn as powerful magic sparked. Stormy skies cleared. The rain stopped. The gloom brightened into a million pinpoint stars. *"Ancient Fae magic. An illusion. Harmless unless provoked, then—"*

"It'll what—eat you?"

"Something like that."

"Terrific."

"Stay sharp, aye?"

"Yeah," Tempel said, green eyes narrowed.

Leveling out, Levin tracked the troop of warnocks through the magical interference. Shimmer danced between tree trunks. Fairy lights sparkled against stone. He shuttered his vision, protecting his light-sensitive eyes from the glow, and searched the terrain ahead.

Thick woodland gave away to a heart-shaped clearing. His mind took a snapshot. A single lane leading in —rough, made muddy by heavy rains, and, given the deep tread marks, recently traveled. Scanning the ground, he looked ahead. One tree with a huge canopy in the middle of the dell, a dozen warnocks milling around something hidden behind branches and big leaves.

Still a quarter mile away, he watched the troop. On the prowl. Circling. Hunting for prey. Impatient to maim. Ready to pull the guts from whatever had been stupid enough to stumble into their territory.

The second the troop found it, the Alpha would eat, throwing tidbits of the hapless victim to the others. After which the remains would be dragged back to their owners. In the same way a cat left dead mice on the floor for the one she loved. An unusual love language. A disgusting one, given warnocks preferred human prey.

Worry trickled in. Aggression rose, streaming through his veins. Levin increased his wing speed. Fifty feet above the valley floor, he scanned right to left, looking for—

"*Shite,*" he growled, seeing the flipped Land Rover.

Huge even by warnock standards, the beast standing on top of the SUV beat its hooves against the undercarriage. Another pushed against the side, sending the mangled truck pirouetting on its roof across ground. Glass shards shrieked against crumpled steel. The twisted metal frame shuddered. His eyes sliced to the cab, and—

"*Goddamn it,*" Tempel growled.

"*Fucking hell,*" Levin said, speaking over his friend, his chest so tight air snagged in his lungs. "*Female, an HE.*"

"*She's trapped inside, Lev.*"

He could see that, along with the unearthly glow.

Pulsing with power, the energy aura came from inside the SUV, spilling out through broken windows, pushing preternatural light across the ground.

He clenched his teeth.

Bad luck.

The absolute worst.

Without her in the mix, his plan didn't change—tag a warnock, follow the troop home, kill the rogue tribe terrorizing the Highlands. With her fucking up his flow, he was screwed. As much as he wanted to, his dragon refused to ignore her. His beast was already fixated, more concerned about her than a missed opportunity to KO the enemy. Annoying, but not all that surprising, given the rarity of her bio-energy. His magical side recognized her importance, reminding him a high-energy female couldn't be wasted, no matter how important the mission.

Males of his kind needed females of her caliber. Ones with a direct connection to the Meridian, source of all living things. Cursed by a vengeful goddess, the connection between Dragonkind and the electrostatic bands ringing the planet lay shattered, making it impossible for him and his brethren to connect and draw the nourishment they needed to stay healthy and strong. Without human females, Dragonkind would slowly starve to death, which meant...

He must intervene. Now. Before the warnocks figured out she sat unmoving inside the truck, aura burning bright, mostly unhurt, though he could smell the tang of her blood in the air.

"Jesus," Tempel said. *"Lev—"*

"I got her."

"We're too far away, man. Those things are gonna—"

"I got her," he said, pushing through the limits of his magic.

The web of ancient Fae magic snarled.

Heat blistered across his scales. Frost melted. Pain

raked him with razor-sharp claws. Pushing the agony to the periphery, Levin blew past safe speeds into supersonic. Space opened in front of him only to snap closed behind him.

A cataclysmic boom echoed.

The truck radio switched on. Static hissed a second before a hard tap came from inside the truck.

Hooves planted on the underside of the SUV, the warnock looked down. Baring two rows of needle-sharp teeth, it punched through the floorboards. Metal shrieked as the beast tore a hole in the heavy truck frame.

The female screamed.

The warnock snarled and, with brute strength and unbelievable speed, yanked the female, still belted into her seat, out into the open. Attached to a piece of twisted steel, hanging upside down, the HE female flailed, scrambling to undo the locking mechanism on the buckle.

The Alpha jumped down and swung the seat full circle, jerking its intended victim around, then stopped, cocked its elbow, and swung hooked claws. Time slowed as the creature's intent became clear. Disembowelment instead of a quick death. Goddess help him. The warnock planned to start eating her while she was still alive.

With a low snarl, Levin conjured his weapons. Magic lashed the air. Long, curved, thin, and deadly, ice daggers materialized in his paws. He threw the first, then unleashed the next. Multiple blades rotated end over end, razor edges hissing through the damp.

A blast of arctic wind blew the wet hair out of the female's face. The glint of a knife zipped between her and the beast.

The icy blade slammed into the warnock, carving flesh to slice through bone. The Alpha jerked backward. Black blood splattered across the HE's chest.

The beast howled.

The severed hand spun away, landing with a thump beside the tree.

With another roar, the warnock dropped her captive. Cradling her stump, the Alpha turned on its hooves and galloped toward the high cliffs.

Left behind, he saw the female suck in a quick breath. Half buried in the mud, the truck seat listed sideways. Panic beating in her aura, the HE snapped her head in his direction. She looked skyward, searching for the one who'd saved her while struggling to free herself from the thick strap locking her in.

His dragon half reacted as she came into focus.

Long, wet hair plastered to her head. Warm hue to her brown skin fueled by the powerful pulse of chilly bio-energy. High cheekbones in an arresting face. Thin scar bisecting one of her eyebrows. A female with eyes so dark the pupils approached black and...

Goddess.

He knew her.

He'd know her anywhere.

Any-fucking-where.

His dream lass. Here. In the middle of nowhere. About to be maimed by a vicious pack of predators, if he didn't get his tail in gear. And yet he couldn't tear his gaze away.

Enthralled, he continued to stare, memorizing her features. Captivated by her brilliance of her bio-energy. Unable to believe what he was seeing, even though he knew he wasn't dreaming, so focused on her face, he lost velocity and wobbled in midair.

Bitter winds rattled over his scales, pushing him off course.

Tempel growled at him.

Levin sucked in a quick breath, got back on track, and let his dragon lead. Flying faster, he closed the distance. He needed to reach her. Before disaster struck, the Alpha regrouped, and—

Running full speed, the troop raced past her. The ground shook. Sound inside the clearing warped. The rainbow disappeared. Stampeding hooves slammed into the mangled SUV. Mud and chunks of grass flew into the air. The truck sliced sideways, hitting the torn pieces of frame his mate sat inside, throwing it toward the tree truck. Levin whispered a command. A snow-drift curled up and over, ready to catch her before she hit the—

Sprinting past, another warnock grabbed, then yanked her seat out of midair.

Her head slammed into the backrest.

With a scream, she dug her heels into the ground, trying to slow the beast down. The warnock kept running, galloping after its companions, taking her on a rough ride toward hidden caves Levin knew he must keep the troop from entering. Otherwise, he'd lose sight of her, and his dream lass would end up dead, buried deep underground, under the watchful eye of dark Druids who called themselves Legion.

7

U nable to believe she was still alive, Priya struggled to undo her seatbelt. An impossible task, given her damaged hand, and the fact she was being dragged at breakneck speed (bottom of her seat attached to part of her ripped-to-shit Rover) by an animal that, she was pretty sure, zoologists didn't know existed.

But never mind her incredulity.

The finer points, along with freaking out, needed to wait.

She wanted her survival instincts, however, to tap the hell in, then get a move-on. Before the nasty, hooved gorilla thing reached its lair and began making her its next meal.

She bounced over a rocky patch. The terrain tilted and whirled. Her teeth clacked together. Tasting blood in her mouth, Priya slammed her heels into the ground. Undeterred by her effort to slow it down, the beast snorted and kept running. Water splashed up, hitting the back of her seat, splattered across her face. Blinking rapid-fire, she cleared her vision, and using her good hand, grabbed the buckle.

Her hand slipped on wet metal.

Panic hit its height, pushing tears into her eyes. As

her chest tightened, she shook her head, watching color undulate over the clearing, her mind chanting, "What the fuck, what the fuck...*whatthefuck!*" A question pierced through the mental barrage, broadcasting inside her head, calling her a fool—why in the hell had she agreed to this? Only a complete idiot agreed to meet someone she'd never met out in the middle of nowhere.

Boot heels carving twin tracks in the dirt, she hammered the button with the side of her fist.

Over. And over...

And over again.

Nothing. No give in the locking mechanism. Little to no give in the belt strapping her to the seat.

God.

She couldn't keep her arms steady or get a solid grip. She needed to use both of her hands. To press. To pull. To get the belt to release enough for her to wiggle free. Throwing herself off the tilt-a-whirl was going to suck, but a cracked skull was better than disembowelment followed by a pack of animals feasting on her. Maybe she'd be dead before they started. An awful thought, but the alternative of being eaten alive was far, *far* worse.

Heart hammering, chest pumping, she twisted in her seat and tried the buckle again. Her crooked fingers straightened and stretched. Pain pierced the fog of terror. She clung to both, using discomfort and fear to focus her, and caught hold of the base of the buckle. The hard plastic cast encasing her hand skittered across slick steel.

She scrambled to keep hold, swearing, hoping, yanking on the strap. Praying the catch released and the bucket seat spat her out.

Galloping at full speed, the beast jerked its arm. The belt tightened another notch. Her chest compressed. Her seat left the ground. Torn steel groaned. The mangled piece of truck frame twisted in midair. Each breath turned to rasps as the back of her skull slammed into the headrest.

More pain. Another burst of speed and—

The bottom of the footboard under her slammed into the ground. As it bounced and her brain burned, an ache spread behind her breastbone. Hopelessness filled the void. Her eyes started to sting. Priya squeezed them closed, feeling the hot well of tears, unable to believe it had come to this—another error in judgment, another bad decision, one that was about to get her killed in a fairy glen.

A place no one would ever find her body.

So much for proving herself. So much for taking the righteous path. So much for believing she could tell the good guys from the bad. Everything was all upside down and backward. So messed up, she could no longer pretend she stood on the side of the angels. God had abandoned her. *Again.* Like always. The world was broken, bent beyond repair. Truth and honor didn't trump evil. The villainous, the monstrously depraved, won as often, if not more, than goodness, justice, and—

A low snarl sounded from somewhere nearby.

Static electricity zipped over her skin.

Heavy snow blew in, painting the clearing winter white.

The creature changed direction so fast it careened sideways. Priya careened along with it, stomach clenching, a scream locked in the back of her throat. Rapid clicking noises rose around her. She heard the thing hiss. She felt its hooves slide and...

The blizzard swirled, forming into a precise pattern.

Time slowed. Her mind focused, snapping pictures like a camera, each moment a still shot rolling frame by frame.

Something big moved inside the squall. The shadow shifted, morphing into scales, spikes, and twisted horns. A flash of dark blue. A snarl accompanied by pure white fangs. She made out the shape of wings and talons. Bright light painted each snowflake in shimmer a second before she saw the eyes—fierce arctic blue, glowing, fixed on her as a creature of myth surged out of the storm.

Priya froze, every muscle locked as awe and incomprehension clashed.

A huge paw with dark, hooked claws reached for her.

Her lungs unlocked, and she sucked in a harsh breath as the dragon, a predator much bigger and badder than the one dragging her, entered the fray.

8

H e almost had her.

Another second, and she'd be in his talons, sitting snug in the palm of his paw.

Wind lashed at his tail as Levin rocketed across the clearing. Treetops edging the dell whipped in protest. The cliff face trembled, rocks falling, cracking into each other as, gaze on the warnock, he counted off the seconds.

The beast changed direction mid-gallop, angling away from him.

Timing his strike, he changed trajectory. Not by a lot. He'd already set his sights. A minor adjustment to perfect his angle, and—

The target on his prey's hide locked in.

His focus tightened another notch. Magic sparked around him. Arctic burn flamed off his spikes, blurring into blizzard conditions. Ice pellets machine-gunned into the ground, then bounced up, pinging off the scales protecting his belly. He sucked in a lungful of frost, then breathed out aggression and reached for her.

Seconds fell into each other, falling too slow, as though the cosmos had switched tracks, flinging time in the opposite direction.

Not wanting to hurt her, he checked his claws,

curving the lethal edges under to keep from cutting her in the grab-and-go.

Unwilling to give up its prize, the warnock veered left.

Trapped in her seat, his female banged along behind it, hair flying all over the place, each breath coming hard. Gaze glued to him, shock firing in the widening of her dark eyes.

Not a promising start. Or the way he wanted her to look at him the first time. Mayhap he shouldn't have dropped the cloaking spell. Mayhap allowing the troop of warnocks see him wasn't the best idea, given he was scaring the shite out of his mate, but...

He couldn't put the genie back in the bottle.

He'd explain the necessity to his female later. Right now, his mission was simple—kill the warnock. Cut his mate free without her feeling the sharp edges of his claws. After that, he'd do what he'd dreamed of for months—wrap his arms around her. Bury his nose in her hair. Revel in the scent and feel of her. Hold her close while he calmed her down.

Curling one wing under, he flipped up and over. The spark of her bio-energy raked across his scales. Hard, chilly, jewel-like...beautifully electric. The energy she possessed was a revelation, the yin to his magical yang, vibrating at the same frequency. This close to touching her, her aura brightened. The starburst reached out to embrace him, connecting with his dragon half, perfecting their energetic fit.

Recognition slid into immediate acceptance.

The need to protect her hit him like a sledgehammer.

With a snarl, Levin spun into another rotation. He flicked the tip of his tail. The bladed spikes nailed the warnock in the neck. A precise strike. The beast's head left its neck, tumbling into open air. Arterial spray arched skyward, tinted green in the glow of his gaze.

The beast's body jerked and began to fall. Warm blood splattered across Levin's chest.

Thrown upward, his mate screamed.

Ignoring the gore coating his scales, he plucked her out of the air on the flyby. His talons curled around her. She yanked on her seatbelt. She kicked, wee boots thrashing, and yelled, "Fuck!"

"Easy, lass." Angling his wings, Levin flipped upright. "Ye're safe. Give me a second. I'll set down and explain."

She jolted as his voice registered. Her mouth opened, then closed. An instant later, she sucked in what sounded like a painful breath and—

"What the fuck? What the fuck? *Whatthefuck!*" she yelled, flailing in the twisted remains of the truck.

"*Jesus Christ,*" Tempel said, tone a combination of incredulous and pissed off.

"*Calm down. I had her the whole way.*"

"*You cut it close, brother, and...*" Tempel trailed off. "*You don't have her yet. She's freaking the fuck out.*"

"*Donnae worry about her. Told you, I got her.*"

"*You keep saying that, but—*"

"*Did you tag one?*"

"*Yeah,*" Tempel said, full of affront. The sound of flapping wings came through mind-speak. The scratch and scrape of claws landing on stone came next. Perched on a ragged outcropping, he tipped his horned head down, staring at a spot at the base of the cliff. "*The last warnock just entered the cave.*"

"*Ye're locked on?*"

"*Of course.*"

"*Good,*" Levin murmured, banking into a wide turn. "*Track and trace. I need a moment tae get her under control.*"

Tempel snorted. "*Something tells me it's going to take more than a moment.*"

An apt observation.

Levin scowled. "*Just do it.*"

The big American huffed. *"You sound like a bad Nike ad."*

"You just canna help yerself, can you?"

"Shake a leg, man," his wing-mate said, flashing huge fangs from two hundred yards away. *"I wanna get underground."*

Of course Tempel did. The earth dragon never missed a chance to bury himself horns-deep in dirt. Or go spelunking.

His mate shouted, threatening to maim him…by all manner of inventive methods.

He blinked.

She yelled another threat.

His mouth curved. Goddess. She was glorious. So beautiful in temper, she mesmerized him. Head tilted, unable to believe his good luck, he watched her anger escalate. She threatened to yank his horns out by the roots. He clenched his teeth to keep from laughing. Nothing about the situation was funny, but he couldn't help it. His relief that her spirit hadn't been damaged by her encounter with the warnocks was too great. And she was so lovely, so unbelievably fierce. In such a state, she left fear behind, forgetting to be afraid of him.

"Lass, settle," he murmured, wishing he knew her name. His back paws touched down. He folded his wings. The webbing met his sides. "You cannae hurt me with a blowtorch. Skewering me with a rusty pike willnae work either. Also, ye're not strong enough tae crack my skull open like a walnut."

"You…you…" Dark eyes alight with fury, she lashed out. Her knuckles whiffed past one of his talons without making contact. Her frustration spiked, making her aura burn bright blue. "Let me go!"

"I will…when you calm down."

"Calm down? Calm down!" she screeched. "Are you out of your mind?"

Good question. Not at all out of bounds, given he found her attitude—and explosive temper—charming.

He wanted to wallow in his fascination with her. Fly her back to the lair. Settle her in by introducing her to his family and the world he inhabited. After that, he would take his time getting to know her—the hours, days, and weeks needed for him to learn about her, and for her to become accustomed to him. He wanted to pamper her, appreciate her, give her all she needed and everything she wanted. But with Tempel waiting and the warnocks running, he couldn't delay. Which left him with no other choice.

He needed to shift forms and touch her with human hands. Soothe her while he helped her accept the situation, and him.

Rushing her went against the grain. As her mate, he wanted to initiate her into his world the right way— slow and steady, with kindness, compassion, and patience. But some things couldn't be helped or avoided.

The mission and continued safety of his pack demanded he follow through without delay. Before Tempel lost the scent along with his ability to track the troop returning to their owners in Legion territory. So instead of slowing things down, Levin sped it up by unleashing his magic.

No warning.

In an instant, he shifted forms. Hard scales and sharp spikes disappeared. Dragon claws morphed into human hands and feet. Muscle undulated, roping around his bones as magic throbbed through him. He shook his head, flipping strands of blond hair out of his eyes. He heard his female suck in a breath. Registering her shock, he conjured a pair of jeans, but nothing else, leaving his chest and feet bare as he set the bucket seat containing her down. Gently. Then he sank to his haunches, palmed one of his ice daggers, and began cutting her loose.

"Oh my God."

"Relax," he said, asking the impossible while he sawed through her seatbelt. The heavy strap pinning her to the backrest loosened.

"Holy shit," she whispered, voice shaky, body taut as she stared at him.

"Calm, lass." Gaze on his task, he set the edge of the blade above the buckle. He sliced. Nylon hissed. "I willnae hurt you. A moment more, and—"

The last of her restraints fell away.

Arching up and back, she launched the seat backward. Her boots flipped up. With a curse, Levin ducked to avoid getting kicked in her head. The back of her seat hit the ground. She rolled out, doing a sideways somersault. Her feet met the ground. Pushing up, she turned to run.

An excellent plan. Well executed, but for one thing.

Her legs buckled. On her hands and knees in the mud, she crawled away from him.

Already on his feet, Levin closed the distance and scooped her up. He tightened his arms around her, anchoring her to his frame. She bucked. Securing his hold, he reeled her back in and, kneeling in the mud, legs spread around her arse, pressed his chest into her back.

"Don't, don't—"

"I'm sorry. Ye're shocked, I know. I hate doing it this way, but ye're safe, *zembāla*," he said, talking to her in Dragonese, hoping the soft sounds of his native tongue would soothe her. He wanted her calm enough to listen —to take in and understand what he needed to tell her. She reared instead. Whispering to her, he contained her with gentle hands, refusing to hurt her even as he thwarted her attempts to break his hold. "Ye're safe... ye're safe...ye're safe with me."

"What's happening? I don't understand what's happening." Muscles quivering, exhaustion rising, she shuddered, breath hitching, heart pounding, head shaking. "Who are you?"

"Levin. And you are?"

"What are you?"

"Dragonkind." Resting his arse against his heels, he held her still, nestling in, sharing his energy, surrounding her with his body. "I'll explain, but first, I need yer name."

"What? I don't… This is… I can't—"

"Yer name, lass."

A harsh exhale puffed from her mouth. She sagged against him. "Priya."

He took her weight with ease, cradling her in his arms. "Priya what?"

"Burman."

"English?"

She nodded.

"From where?"

"London."

"Good, *zembāla*. Settle. It's all right."

"No, it's not. It's not. I'm gonna… I'm gonna be… sick."

"Breathe, Priya," he said, moving from captor to shield as her bio-energy buzzed around him. Fae magic was intense. So was his, and as a high-energy female, Priya was more sensitive than most, absorbing more than her system could handle. Toss in the extreme fear caused by the warnock attack and she was standing on a precipice, about to fall into emotional overload. "Yer stomach will settle in a minute."

"L-Levin."

"Right here."

Another shudder racked her small frame. Coiled tight for too long, her muscles gave out. Her will to fight went with it. She made a low sound, and his heart bled for her. So much upheaval, all of it incomprehensible to her.

Her arse in his lap, he kept his arm wrapped over her chest. Cupping her shoulder with one hand, he slid his other hand along the inside of her forearm. His fingertips grazed her pulse point, then brushed over her palm. Priya hesitated. He murmured to her. Like dominoes falling, her spine softened one vertebra at a time as she relaxed, giving him a gift by unclenching her hand. With a hum, he laced his fingers through hers, pressing up until webbing of his hand met hers.

"Shit," she rasped.

"Breathe," he whispered against the top of her head. Staying still and quiet, he held her, giving her time. She exhaled. He breathed her in. Icy, cool scent. She smelled like spearmint and cold winter days. The perfect combination, soothing as fuck and arousing as hell. Curled around her, Levin turned his face into her wet hair. "I've got you, Priya. I've got you—just breathe."

Breathe.

Guidance he should follow himself, as the beauty of her threatened to overcome his control. Priya Burman. His mate. His dream lass. The female made and meant for him. Nestled in his arms. Learning to trust him one breath at a time. Giving him a gift much greater than any he'd received in two hundred years of living.

Gratitude pushed into humbleness.

He closed his eyes and thanked his lucky stars. Along with Shell. The werewolf had given his life, proving Levin and everyone else wrong. The male had cared about *something*. Levin now held her in his arms. All he needed to do now was push past the barriers he sensed deep inside her, make her a part of his world, then convince her to stay.

9

Sitting on her ass in the mud, Priya absorbed the quiet like a sponge. She needed the stillness, that little bit of calm after the storm. While time held its breath. She didn't need it to pause long, a minute or two, just enough to catch her breath.

After that, she'd work on clearing her mind.

Critical, to her way to thinking, given a guy she didn't know sat behind her, holding her tight.

She felt him everywhere. Strong arm angled across her breastbone. Wide chest pressed against her back. Knees in the dirt, the insides of his thighs hugging the outside of hers.

She should've been uncomfortable. Cold. Wet. Completely distraught under the circumstances. Something about his hold, though—solid, yet gentle, close without being invasive—steadied her. Quiet spiraled into charred mental places. Her mind flickered like a light bulb being switched on and off, turning her thoughts into fragments.

Concentrating on the only thing that felt real, she tuned into him. She registered each of his breaths and heard nothing but him. Felt nothing but him. Wanted no one else but him, abandoning the idea she should fight, drawing on his strength, absorbing his calm, experiencing the steady beat of his heart.

Running would've been a smarter choice. Asking questions might be wise too.

Priya ignored those options.

She sat still and silent instead, chest hitching, brain glitching, trusting Levin to support her as she struggled to pull herself back together.

He murmured. Incredible accent, a lovely collection of soft sounds in a language she didn't understand. Listening to him, though, helped. As he talked, composure returned, infiltrating her jumbled thoughts, pouring through her veins like a waterfall over rocks.

The tension constricting her chest eased.

Her heart rate slowed. The jagged pieces of her mind reorganized. Her frayed senses smoothed out. Awareness chased a strange sizzle over her skin. She took a shallow breath, then managed to draw in a deeper one. The first few caught at the back of her throat. Staring straight ahead, not seeing much, she forced air into her lungs and pushed it out.

A tremor juddered through her.

Levin squeezed her hand.

Her fingertips started to tingle.

She glanced down. As though they had a will of their own, her fingers flexed between his much bigger ones. Unable to believe she was holding his hand, she stared at her fingertips. Prickles drew lazy circles across her palm where his skin met hers.

The gentle pulse along with the connection registered. Sensation rolled through her, cresting like a wave. Drifting in the ebb and flow, Priya settled into the stream. A warm, soothing rush. An infusion of some kind. One that plucked at the knots twisting her muscles, freeing her from the tangle.

The rigidity in her spine softened.

Bending her knees, Priya planted her heels and

leaned back, pressing into him instead of away. She needed more. More warmth. More calm. More of the rich current moving from him into her.

"That's it, *zembāla*."

His voice rumbled through her. Thick Scottish accent, low tone.

Her eyes drifted closed. Priya blinked them back open. "What's it mean?"

"*Zembāla?*"

"Yeah."

"My treasure."

She breathed through another shudder. "Like—I was lost and now I'm found."

His mouth curved, brushing her ear. "Something like that."

"I think, maybe, I've gone slightly insane."

"Nay." Giving her a squeeze, he leaned forward, taking her with him. With gentle hands, he shifted her in his arms, then lifted until she sat sideways in his lap. "You've been given a fright. Only natural for it throw you."

Kneeling ass to heels in the dirt, he arranged her legs over the top one of his thighs. She watched him do it without saying a word. She should be protesting. Ought to be pushing him away, but—

He cupped her cheek.

She sucked in a breath as his thumb nudged her chin, tilting her face up. Snowy-blue eyes met hers. A deep sense of recognition burned through her. Incomprehension struck. Surprise tolled like a bell, and yet her mind insisted she knew him, but...

That was impossible.

She didn't know him. Had never laid eyes on him before. And she would remember. No one forgot seeing a man like him.

Men would instinctively give him a wide berth.

Women would flock to his side, hoping to gain his undivided attention.

Held in his thrall, she let her gaze roam his features. Overlong dark blond hair on the messy side. Thick brows over eyes so light his irises looked colorless. Angular cheekbones. A square jaw covered by a beard so well trimmed Priya suffered a keen visceral reaction. She wanted to run her fingers through his whiskers to see what they felt like against her skin.

Bristly and rough? Or soft, on the lighter side of scratchy?

Her belly hollowed out. Tingles swirled toward hipbones. Curling her fingers, she pressed her fists into her stomach, quelling the urge to touch him.

His eyes crinkled at the corners. "I like the look of you too, lass."

"I didn't—"

He raised a brow.

The denial stalled on the tip of her tongue. Intuition sparked, telling her to abandon the argument and hightail it out of dangerous territory. "Ah, guess I freaked out, huh?"

"A wee bit, aye."

"Sorry about that." Her voice cracked. She cleared her throat. "I'm usually better under pressure."

"What happened tae change that?"

Good question. But no way was she going to answer it. She didn't want to talk about the attack that nearly took her life two years ago. Or the fact she'd lost her nerve. Along with her ability to read a situation.

"Long story," she said, praying he left well enough alone.

"One I'm eager tae hear you tell."

"What kind of animals were those?" she asked, changing the subject.

"Dodge all you like, lass, but I see the scars on yer skin. Sense the healed fractures underneath too."

His gaze dropped to her throat. He raised his hand. She tensed as he traced the thin line over her carotid artery with a fingertip. A light touch, yet recall surfaced, making her relive that night. She still felt the blade against her skin. Remembered the sting and suffered the phantom pain.

Levin made a low noise. His hand dropped to wrap around the plastic cast on her wrist. The gel inside reacted to his touch, moving from cool to hardcore cold.

She sighed in relief.

His expression softened. "Believe me when I say we'll get into it later."

"Nothing to get into. Car accident, that's all."

"Bullshite."

She clenched her teeth. No way was she talking about it. Not with him, or anyone else. She'd spent enough time thinking about the trafficking ring and the thug who'd been sent to stop her from writing her story. Nothing good would come from rehashing the past. She'd moved on.

Her chest tightened a notch.

At least, she was *trying* to move on. Reliving the night that changed her life would only cause her more pain.

"You don't know anything."

"I've got a brain in my head, eyes tae see, and magic for the rest, Priya," he said, refusing to allow her deflection. "Lying tae me willnae get you the result you want."

Desperate to move him off topic, she ignored the warning. "Magic?"

"Dragonkind, remember?"

The reminder careened though her mind like a bowling ball knocking down pins. As the clatter echoed, an image formed on her mental screen. White, blue and gray scales. Huge talons tipped by lethal-looking claws. The glow of shimmering, snowy eyes. The same pair staring into hers as Levin held her gaze.

His intensity beat against her disbelief, issuing a clear challenge—*ignore the truth at your own peril.*

A quiver speared down her spine.

She swallowed past the lump in her throat. "You're a dragon."

"Half."

"What?"

"The rest of what makes me is human," he said, delivering the news with such nonchalance, Priya blinked like a startled owl. "The species that comprise Magickind are many and varied. Dragonkind is a unique subset, the most powerful, able tae shift forms at will."

"How can that be?" she asked, her voice faint.

"You'll learn, in the grand scheme of things, humans donnae know much. Yer race, lass..." Levin shook his head. "Self-centered, selfish tae the point of obliviousness. Humankind does damage without caring who it hurts."

Difficult to argue, given climate change and the state of global politics. Still...

"I don't... I can't even... What am supposed to do with that?"

He shrugged. "Accept it."

"Accept it?"

"Easier that way. Less hassle."

Raking her hair back, she fisted her hand in the strands. Gaze glued to his, she held the wet mess in a bunch against the top of her head. "I feel a migraine coming on."

He chuckled. "I'm not surprised."

She scowled at him. "Right. Okay, well, hard to argue, since I've seen your dragon half, so...moving on. You didn't answer my other question."

"Which one?"

"What were those things?"

"Warnocks."

"Where did they come from?"

"I'll answer yer questions, Priya, any you care tae ask, but not now. Time's wasting, and Tempel's—"

A knock reverberated.

Her attention snapped to the side. Priya blinked, then looked up and around, thinking, *What in the hell?* A question she should've asked earlier, given she sat at the center of a snow globe. A perfect sphere carved from ice, glassy smooth on the inside, frosted on the outside. A shadow stood outside it, feet planted, hand raised, knuckles banging against the hard exterior.

Each rap echoed inside the globe.

Priya flinched.

"Fuck," Levin murmured.

"Please tell me that's a friend."

"Pain in the arse, more like, but Tempel's right tae be impatient." His arms tightened around her. Rocking backward, he pushed to his feet. A second later, she stood teetering on unsteady legs beside him. Brushing her hair aside, he wrapped his hand around her nape, keeping her upright, then turned toward the man-shaped silhouette outside the globe. "We need tae move. Get into the caves."

"Caves?"

"Cannae track the warnocks from the air, lass. Need tae be underground tae hunt the troop. No time tae fly you back tae the lair, and I cannae leave you in the dell. 'Tisn't safe," he said as though going after a pack of vicious predators was a perfectly normal thing to do. "So, ye're coming with me."

Her brows popped toward her forehead. "Are you crazy?"

"Nay."

Grabbing her hand, he tugged her along behind him as he walked toward the edge of the sphere. The shadow standing beside it moved away. Levin murmured. The temperature dropped. Breathing out white puffs with each exhale, she watched the frost crystals swirl in front of him. Ice melted. The sphere disappeared as, boot soles squishing through the mud, Levin strode after the guy jogging ahead of them, making for the high cliffs edging the clearing.

"You are," she said, feet moving triple time to keep up with him. "You're crazy."

He grinned.

"This is kidnapping."

"You wanna stay here—" He threw her sideways glance. "—alone?"

Priya bit her lip, then looked over her shoulder. Her ripped-to-shreds, beyond-all-repair Rover came into view. Fine hairs rose, standing straight up on the back of her neck. She swallowed her retort as her mouth went dry.

No way in hell.

She wasn't saying in the clearing, not for any reason, which meant she was stuck.

Smack dab in the middle of a mess with no hope of digging herself out. About to follow a couple of dragon guys into a cave where a pack of vicious predators lived...and would no doubt try to eat her again.

10

P erched on Levin's back, Priya hung on, arms around his neck, legs gripping his hips as he sprinted after Tempel. His friend, dragon buddy… whatever. Labels didn't mean anything right now. The aggressive vibe expanding inside the underground tunnel mattered a whole lot more.

Pinpricks tapped across her cheekbones. Tingles drew circles on her temples, then turned and needled down her spine.

The sound of pounding footfalls raged around her. Her ability to focus on anything else took a hit. Levin's speed was unbelievable, the stuff of madcap imaginations spun into monster-inspired fairytales, as the terrain blurred and her senses burned.

Dragons who could turn into men.

Warnocks, a veritable nightmare come to life, and…

Who knew what else? Were there gargoyles around the next corner? What about a horde of cannibalistic Minotaurs?

The questions banged around inside her head. She inhaled a choppy breath.

As the exhale shuddered from her throat, Levin increased the pace. Her grip on him weakened, then slipped. As she listed sideways, Priya fisted her good hand in the front of his t-shirt, right over his heart. Hitching her other elbow, she sliced her weak one down, then up, pressing the inside of forearm in a diagonal across his chest.

Without breaking stride, Levin grabbed hold. Big hand. Strong grip. His fingers flexed around the plastic cast protecting her damaged hand. He squeezed. She braced, expecting pain. Frost swirled around her wrist. The gel pads against her skin chilled. Cold sank through her sore muscles to reach her once-broken bones, delivering relief instead of agony.

Her breathing moved from ragged to smooth. Her heartbeat leveled out as panic downgraded, taking her from freaked out to somewhat focused. Blinking away the grit in her eyes, she stared at the bottom of Tempel's boot heels.

Less than a car length away, the guy ran at break-neck speed. Dodging rocky outcroppings, he navigated tight turns, long legs churning, green eyes glowing with the same intensity as Levin's light blue ones.

Her mind catalogued the moment. Big guy, built strong, taller than Levin, but not by much.

She'd been introduced to Tempel on the fly, mere seconds before Levin picked her up and started running. The very definition of a fast exchange. Lots of fury and movement before moonlight faded and the damp confines of the cave closed in. A slash of an instant, long enough for her to understand life had changed in a major way. And also that resistance (along with arguing) was futile.

Not that she hadn't tried to speak up.

Levin answered each time, though his responses stayed short. He muttered things like *later*, *hold on*, and her all-time favorite, *quiet, zembāla*. His bossiness lit the fuse on her temper, making her want to smack him upside the head. A tempting thought. Completely counterproductive, given his speed, and the fact she didn't want to fall, but...

God. Seriously—how could she not say anything?

The entire situation landed somewhere south of insane.

She didn't understand any of it. Levin acted as though she weighed nothing. Knees firing like pistons, he ran without restraint, his form perfect, unhindered by the fact he carried her like a backpack. A live, woman-sized one with her fair share of curves.

Flattening her palm against his chest, she felt his chest rise and fall. Even breaths. Steady heartbeat. Muscles bunching and releasing, no sweat on his skin.

Incredible. Incomprehensible. *Inhuman.*

The last she picked up without difficulty. Given what she'd seen (and he told her in the clearing), the dragon-man aspect came in for a bumpy landing inside her mind. She ought to be terrified, and yet, even in the midst of her fear, curiosity took over. She had so many questions. So very little made sense, though...

She'd managed to nail down a few details since the insanity began—supernatural dragon guys possessed a serious amount of focus. Toss in raptor-like intensity, strong wills, and edgy natures, and she got the message.

She was along for the ride.

Levin wasn't going to stop.

The realization left her with two options. One, hang on as instructed. And two, start praying she was still alive when the crazy train stopped, and Levin let her go.

Her stomach dipped on the thought. Convincing him she wasn't a threat—that she could keep her mouth shut—amounted to a long shot. The worst kind of wishful thinking, optimism taken too far after what she'd witnessed.

Priya wasn't stupid or naïve. She was a grownup living in the real world. She'd seen what she'd seen, happenings instinct warned her human beings never saw. It didn't take a genius to figure out Levin might lock her up and throw away the key.

Unease uncoiled inside her. "Shit."

"Relax."

"You relax," she said through clenched teeth.

"I will—later, when ye're asleep beside me in bed."

The leash on her temper snapped.

She opened her mouth to—

Levin dodged right, then veered left, moving so fast the protest stalled in the back of her throat. Outrage made her try again. She got the same result, losing her ability to breathe as he sliced through a series of twists and turns, charging after a bunch of warnocks who didn't know they were being chased.

Yet.

Yes, *yet*...that needed to be made clear. Stated in plain language, maybe even broadcast in CAPITAL LETTERS. Not to her. She understood the danger while Levin and his pal ignored it. Unaffected by an idiotic plan, the dynamic duo embraced their inner kamikazes, dragging her into the middle of their death wish.

Buzzing joined the hammer of heavy footfalls.

A golden glow ate through the darkness behind her.

Priya looked over her shoulder. "Levin—"

"Earth dragon magic."

"What—"

Fireflies hurtled around a bend in the tunnel.

Her mouth fell open as the swarm flew in behind her. Bumping into each other and the ceiling, hundreds of insects streamed overhead, tumbling after Tempel. Levin's eyes added to the light parade. The blue glow of his gaze intensified, illuminating jagged walls, allowing her to see every dip and hollow in the system of interconnected caves.

The tunnel took a sharp turn.

The gradient changed, becoming steeper. The terrain shifted underfoot, becoming rougher. Gray granite transitioned to black stone shot through with thick veins of white and gold crystals.

Pretty any other time, but—

Levin dodged a jagged outcropping. She wobbled on his back as he powered up a steep rise toward what look like a dead end.

Boots slamming against stone, Tempel disappeared around the bend.

The swarm followed.

As the golden light parade faded, Levin rocketed through the narrow opening. Sharp stone came an inch from slamming into her head. Dust blew into her face. Dirt washed into her mouth.

Choking on grit, Priya coughed and squeezed his neck. "Levin—"

"Tuck," he growled without missing a stride.

Another order.

Anger spiked, reigniting her temper. "Listen—"

"Now, Priya."

She frowned at the back of his head. Her gaze flicked up. The tunnel ceiling overhead dipped. She ducked, pressing her face into the back of his neck as fear pushed anger out of the way. An odd quake started inside her. The ripple effect rumbled through her, shaking self-preservation loose.

Arguing with Levin was a bad idea. Antagonizing him was an even worse one. He was bigger, much stronger, than her. He owned fangs, scales, and a set of claws that put all other predators to shame, so…

Quiet and compliant—self-preservation at its best, capitulation at its worst. The idea left a bad taste in her mouth. She despised the feeling. Hated her helplessness too. It felt wrong to let fear lead, to hand her power over to another. To rely on Levin without first knowing if she could trust him.

"You can trust me," he growled, taking another sharp turn.

"Sorry?"

"You can, Priya."

"Oh my God," she whispered against his neck. "Can you… Are you—"

"Reading yer mind?"

"That's impossible."

"Not for me. Not when it comes tae us," he said. "The bond is strong. Took hold fast, lass. A matched set…mated. I have access tae you now."

She shook her head.

"I'll prove it tae you."

An odd rap tapped on her temples. A cool, pleasing sensation swirled over her shoulders, dragging tingles to the surface of her skin. Something clicked inside her. Her mind expanded, opening into areas she'd never felt before.

Levin hummed.

"That's you."

"*All me. You felt me before,*" he said, deep voice sounding in the spaces he now occupied inside her mind. "*Now, you hear me too.*"

Her good hand flexed in his t-shirt. "That's—"

"*Magic. Energy-fuse. As real as it gets.*"

"I don't want anything to do with…" She paused. "Whatever it is. In fact, I don't want anything to do with any of this."

"*Too late now.*"

"Not if I kill you."

He huffed, the sound full of amusement. "*Hang on.*"

"Shut up!"

His chuckle echoed through the corridors of her mind. Lifting her head, she called him a nasty name.

He planted his boot on a ledge. His muscles coiled.

His spine arched. Gravity lightened as he launched himself (and her) over a deep gorge. Wind slapped her in the face. Blurred light flickered across the dark surface of a serpentine river below. A scream caught in the back of her throat.

Clearing the expanse, he slammed his feet down.

She jolted.

He powered up another steep rise.

Each stride jolted through her. Gritting her teeth, she tried to tighten her grip. An impossibility. She was already exerting maximum strength. Not that Levin noticed. He continuing running, paying her no mind at all. Except...

She frowned. That wasn't quite true.

He wasn't ignoring her. He continued to talk—telling her it would be all right, assuring her she was safe, being comforting in ways she didn't want to contemplate.

"*Almost there,* zembãla."

"Almost where?"

"*The warnocks are less than a quarter mile ahead.*"

"Terrific," she mumbled. "I've always wanted one for Christmas."

Levin snorted in amusement, then explained, "*Get ready, lass. The second I exit the cave, it'll happen fast.*"

"What's going to happen?"

"*Once I'm in dragon form, I'll find a safe place tae stash you, then—*"

"Stash me?" she asked, hearing the squeak in her voice.

"*Cannae take you into battle, Priya,*" he said, sounding so reasonable she wanted to hit him. Again. For the thousandth time in less than half an hour.

Had to be a record.

Not that she could dwell on it. She had bigger problems ahead. "You're not stashing me anywhere."

"*You want tae get eaten?*"

A threat.

Her stomach cramped. "No."

"Then prepare tae be stashed."

A warning.

Her mind churned.

Priya forced her chaotic thoughts into some semblance of order. Panic wouldn't help her. She needed to think…focus and figure it out. Identifying the variables topped the list of things to tackle. After that, she'd solidify the details of her plan. *Be quick. Be decisive. Be smart.* Three pillars of an excellent strategy. One she could execute independent of Levin and his mission.

Taking a fortifying breath, she raised her head. Her gaze tracked over his hair, up the broken pathway. Jagged walls illuminated by bumbling fireflies. The wide expanse of Tempel's back. The echo of hooves striking stone. Snorts and lows growls joined the cacophony, sending symphonic layers of percussion up the tunnel.

Her heart started to keep time. As each beat pounded the inside of her breastbone, the dizzying height of her disbelief grew. How had meeting a source devolve into, well…*this?* Dragons and energy-fuse. Warnocks and Druids. An investigative reporter out of her depth. A tragicomedy in the making.

She wanted to blame Levin for her confusion. For the mess and fear that followed. For thrusting her into a strange world where magic ruled and strange creatures roamed. For landing her in a place she didn't understand and knew wasn't safe.

A stretch toward self-pity. He was, after all, an easy target. Too bad a strong sense of fairness refused to let her do it.

None of this was his fault.

He'd saved her life, pulled her from the danger she placed herself in, so…no. Blaming him wasn't fair. She'd failed to do her due diligence, trusted Shell too soon. Had been too invested in the outcome, wanted the story too much. As difficult as it was to admit, she'd created the problem and deserved whatever nastiness came her way.

"*Stop it, Priya,*" Levin murmured, tone warm with understanding. "*No harm will come tae you. I willnae allow it.*"

"I really need you to shut up."

He turned his head. His beard brushed her face as he gifted her with his profile. Straight white teeth flashed as he grinned.

"It isn't funny."

"*Ye're right, zembāla. It isnae. But instead of beating yerself bloody, think of it this way...*" His voice tapered off, going silent inside her mind. Returning his gaze to the path, he reached up and over. His hand landed light, but firm, curling around the base of her skull. Chilly wisps brushed over her nape. A strong current trickled down her spine. The worries plaguing her faded. Comfort took its place, making her feel safe, helping her trust him more. "*If you'd refused tae meet Shell, you wouldn't have been there for me tae find. I've been searching a long time, lass. I donnae care how you've come tae me—I'm just so fucking happy that you have.*"

Well...

Shit.

What was she supposed to say to that? Particularly since she didn't understand what he meant. She was missing information. Nothing about Levin made sense. Everything about him felt right. The dichotomy spoke to her, even as it twisted her into knots.

Shale tumbled down the hill in front of them.

Stone cracked against stone, echoing as Tempel slowed from sprint to jog. Bathed in moonlight, he settled into a crouch at the top of the rise, and glanced over his shoulder, triumph shining in his green eyes.

Levin growled in return.

Halfway up, the mouth of a cave came into view.

Stopping on the lip, Levin swung her off his back and hit his haunches next to Tempel. Settled in the cove created by the spread of his knees, she watched warnocks thunder down the side of the mountain, hooves kicking up dust. She tensed. Levin gave her a gentle squeeze, then pointed with his free hand, drawing her attention to the valley below.

Moonlight cast a sliver hue, gliding the treetops, painting the forest floor before touching down on a collection of small cottages. Chimneys smoking gently. Foundations planted close to a wide, fast-moving river. A community nestled deep in the wildness, shaded by old-growth trees and steep rock rising to meet mountain peaks.

A million questions flew into her head.

Priya collected each one, trying to decide which to ask first, but—

Levin hadn't lied. The shift happened fast.

One moment she sat between the spread of his thighs. The next, she lay in center of a giant dragon paw covered in icy scales. Huge talons flexed. Lethal-looking claws hinged inward.

She gasped, then ducked to avoid being impaled.

Levin bared enormous fangs, then unfolded his wings.

"Jesus!"

"*Relax*, zembāla."

"Go to hell, Levin."

Green scales winking in the low light, Tempel laughed.

Levin shook his horned head and, with an acrobatic twist, launched himself upward. Her stomach pitched. Sharp claws caught against solid rock. Spiked tail flying into view, he started to climb the vertical cliff face.

"I don't want to be stashed."

"*I donnae care.*"

"What if you don't come back?"

"I'll come back." Reaching a wide ledge, he hopped onto the flat expanse. A wind gust raked over the outcropping. A clump of snow whipped off the edge. Eyes the color of arctic tundra met hers through the space between his talons. *"Good a place as any."*

Priya stared at him in horror. A second later, she tore her gaze away to look up and down. Mountain peaks above her. Sheer drop and certain death below her. No way off the ledge if he left her here.

"No way," she whispered.

"Be good," he said, setting her down, back pressed to the mountainside.

Her legs gave out. As her ass touched down on solid rock, ice formed around her, walling her off, hemming her in, blocking out the wind. The air stilled. The temperature shifted from cold to comfortable. Fog rose, swirling over the floor. A chair made of ice materialized inside her makeshift prison. A stack of books, along with a water bottle and a box of chocolate-covered biscuits, slid in beside it.

Her mouth fell open.

Anger rippled through her.

Pushing to her feet, she yelled at the wall, "Fuck you!"

"Looking forward tae that, lass."

"Oh my God!" she shouted, voice echoing in the ice cave, unable to believe his nerve.

Not that it mattered.

Her exasperation was irrelevant. Levin was already gone.

11

Fighting the urge to gut someone, Callas drifted across the night sky. Minutes filled with nothing but slow and steady. Hours spent in flight, trailing the Danish pack, with little to show for it.

New night, weeks of the same old shit.

No new information. No interesting insights. Not a single drop of blood on his claws.

A sad state of affairs.

Breathing deep, he exhaled slow. Steam twisted up from his nostrils. With a swipe of his webbed paw, he cleared the mist from his visual field. He should've guessed it would go bad. Playing spy wasn't his forte. Attacking his prey, killing quick and clean, suited him better. Shock and awe, the whiplash of surprise, worked for him too. Trailing a rogue pack from one location to another without making himself known, however—not so much.

Five miles ahead of him, the Danes banked east, flying out of human-controlled territory. Fields and farmland became foothills rolling toward thick forest and the Grampian mountain range. The pack slowed as a unit. Grizgunn's light blue scales flashed in weak moonlight. The Danish commander hovered in midair a beat.

Tilting his wings, Callas gained altitude, stretching five miles to six. Thick clouds enveloped him. He tweaked his magic, amping the wattage. Damp air turned into rain showers. Fat droplets splattered over his shark-gray scales. The razor-sharp blade riding his spine quivered as he tightened the cloaking spell keeping him hidden from view.

A good call.

Grizgunn wasn't an idiot. Proof positive lay in the fact the male had taken one look at Callas in the back garden of Holyroodhouse and said, "No fucking way." Well, not literally, but the words had been written all over the asshole's face.

Grizgunn didn't want Callas anywhere near his pack. Not as a member, or even as a friend who nibbled around the edges.

Another frustrating setback, given his mission, but not altogether unexpected.

He was a strong male. A water dragon who commanded powerful magic. Once a gifted leader, now nothing but a pawn in Silfer's twisted game.

The idea, his entrapment by the Dragon God, hit him like a punch to the gut. It always did. But tonight wasn't about regrets. He needed to stay focused and on point. For the first time in weeks, Grizgunn was off pattern. Instead of sticking close to the city center, he was flying into the middle of nowhere, risking detection by the Scottish pack in open sky. Not a lot of places for the asshole to hide. Even fewer for him to run.

An interesting observation that spelled trouble. The good kind, the sort Callas could get behind.

His eyes narrowed on the Danes. *Kólasi*, he hoped something happened tonight. He needed a break. A way in, something that would push him closer to getting what he wanted—a meeting with Cyprus, commander of the Scots. Not an easy get. He'd been trying since he flew into the male's territory, using back channels—email and forums used by Dragonkind buried in the dark net—to contact the next pack on his list.

He needed to lay eyes on the warriors Cyprus commanded. Check off the box and move on if none of the Scots proved to be the one Silfer wanted him to find.

Adjusting his wing speed, Grizgunn changed his trajectory. The contingent ahead of him stayed on course. A disturbance echoed to the north, pushing invisible rings across the sky and—

Three males sliced into view, and…

Fifteen warriors became eighteen.

A large gathering of Dragonkind. An impressive sight. Every color of the rainbow represented. Not that he cared about the dizzying array of scaly splendor. Though it certainly was interesting.

Grizgunn hadn't been idle in the last month. He'd been busy recruiting, adding to his pack, promising stray males a home, offering a bounty for the assassination of the warriors in Cyprus's pack.

Callas had heard the rumors in Edinburgh. Now, he saw the proof, watching the Danes split into groups of three, forming six fighting triangles. Perfect precision executed by a single unit. Aerial organization practiced for a purpose.

His sonar pinged as individual rogues blipped onto his radar.

Wanting a closer look, Callas conjured his eye in the sky. A vertical pool of water materialized in front of him. Magic pierced the rippling surface, slicing through the center like an arrow. His vision tunneled. Salt water morphed into a curved magnifying glass. He pushed the powerful lens, the size of a drone, across the sky. As it zipped over woodland toward the distant mountain range, he brought the lens in behind the rogue pack.

It ghosted in their wake.

The Danes didn't notice. No one ever did.

Silent, invisible, fast in flight, the lens gave him more than just a dragon's-eye view. It provided close-contact details while he remained miles away. A useful skill, a talent as rare as his subset of Dragonkind. The lens allowed him to see everything, slicing in behind the Danes, hunting like a submarine did a warship—from below the surface of the sea.

Falling back, he watched from beyond the ten-mile maker.

Grizgunn and his pack banked north, then swung east. The pack flew up, over and around rough terrain. Quick turns turned into a series of slow rolls. Callas flexed his talons, trying to stay patient as frustration rose.

"*Kólasi*," he grumbled, swearing in Greek, wishing he was back home on Crete, instead of here...following a bunch of assholes who never did anything interesting. "Waste of precious time."

A lesser male would stop. Admit defeat. Get off the insane merry-go-round, close down the investigation, forget about the past, and restart his life.

The familiar litany jabbed at him.

Callas locked it down, refusing to listen to his darker angels. The lighter ones, though, sat on his shoulder, spoon-feeding him hope. Some night, somewhere, he'd find what he was looking for. Unearth a tidbit of information. Stumble onto a clue that pointed to another. He didn't need much. A hint. A direction. A place to start. Someone willing to give him the answers he needed to right a decades-old wrong and heal the open wound to his heart.

A dream too big to be realized, maybe, but...

He would never stop searching for his son. Never quit hoping he found the infant he'd sired thirty-five years ago. Memories of the night he learned of the pregnancy lashed at him. His chest started to hurt. Images of a different time and place flashed in his mind's eye. The ocean swims. The sound of her laughter. The light in her eyes when she looked at him.

Controlling the lens, Callas kept tabs on the Danes, ghosting across a valley, drifting over mountain peaks while recall battered him. He breathed through the pain. Goddess, his Amelia. Decades later, and he still missed her. She'd been so beautiful. His match. His mate. The North Star in a sky that had been dark before he met her...and burned bright afterward.

Her death dimmed his world again.

He felt dead inside without her—cruel and unfeeling, destructive and vindictive, a male driven by nothing but his mission. And yet he remembered everything about her.

Every second spent. Every kiss shared. Every secret revealed.

He'd clung to his memories of her for years. Wouldn't have survived imprisonment without her voice in his ear, without recall replaying his nights with her over and over inside his head. The need to fight for their son kept him going—then and now—helping him withstand the crippling slash of isolation and hang on to the tattered edges of his mind.

Desperation did that to a male.

So did having a cause.

Grizgunn and his pack of marauding thugs provided an excellent one. The perfect entry point, the excuse he needed to dig in and hunker down until he managed to meet with Cyprus. Nothing but a ruse, a well-honed lie designed to determine one thing— whether Silfer's son made his home among the Scots.

Once Callas sat down with Cyprus, he'd know one way or the other. Either the warrior he hunted lived with the Scots, or he didn't. The second he laid eyes on the male, he'd do one of two things—make a positive

ID or inform Silfer his son wasn't in Scotland and move on to investigate another Dragonkind pack.

Rinse.

Repeat.

Until he hand-delivered the Dragon God's offspring, and Callas received the name and location of his own son in return.

Should be easy. Problem was...

Simplicity never arrived with Silfer in the mix.

Chaos was the deity's preferred brand of poison—and hope a deft weapon. He wielded hope like a knife the second he'd freed Callas from the steel sarcophagus anchored to the bottom of the ocean floor. Cursed by a sea witch, he'd spent years trapped inside an underwater crypt in the lost city of Atlantis, paying for crimes not his own. Days, weeks, months...decades of torment, delivered by a hag who refused to believe Callas wanted, and planned to mate, someone else.

Fury balled in the center of his chest.

He wanted to rage at Silfer...point the finger and shift the blame. Reality refused to let him. He'd put himself here, accepting what the Dragon God offered, making a deal with the devil for his freedom...for the chance to meet his son.

No sense denying it.

Beauregard and Rune didn't even try. The warriors he called brothers hadn't liked the deal he'd struck then any better than they did now. Then again...what had he said? Ah, yes. *Desperation.* Anguish and despair explained a lot. The need to find his son accounted for even more. Which made him the worst kind of fool. Desperate males made idiotic decisions that, almost always, rolled downhill into disaster.

Flying off his right wingtip, Rune tapped him with the side of his tail. Eyes the color of mercury met his. Callas shook his head, warning his friend to leave well enough alone.

Static hissed through mind-speak.

A knock sounded inside his head.

Glaring at his friend, Callas bared his fangs. A warning, the one he always issued when he didn't want to talk about it. He'd already said too much, been too selfish, dragging his brothers-in-arms into his mess, putting both on Silfer's radar. A place smart males knew to avoid. And yet Rune and Beauregard hadn't hesitated when he laid out the plan. The second Callas explained, both males suited up, taking his back, putting themselves at risk, and—

The rapping turned to loud hammering.

Callas sighed. Fucking Rune. The male never left well enough alone. Avid communicators, silver dragons rarely ever did, and Rune wasn't an exception to the rule.

His brother-in-arms hammered him again.

The connection whiplashed as he flipped a mental switch.

A deep voice with a Moroccan accent streamed through mind-speak. *"You're spiraling."*

Callas shook his head.

"Bullshite," Rune said, challenging him, like always. *"I warned you, Cal. You went down that rabbit hole, I'd dig in."*

"I'm good, brother. Just rethinking our strategy." Rolling his shoulders, Callas attacked the tension. Taut muscles squawked. Pain flickered down his spine. *"This one isn't working."*

"Halle-fucking-lujah," Beauregard said, French accent laced with impatience. And no small amount of sarcasm, a dry wit honed in the South of France. Though Callas couldn't be sure of the location. His friend was secretive to the point of paranoid. The male never spoke of the past. *"About time you started talking sense."*

Rune frowned. *"Beau—"*

Beauregard huffed. *"I mean, come on. What the hell are we doing?"*

Callas sighed. *Good question.* Especially since he wasn't sure anymore.

Frost spiraled into snowflakes as Beauregard growled, "*Seriously,* mon ami—*what the fuck? I could 've killed Grizgunn ten times by now. Then flipped him over and killed him some more. What're you waiting for?*"

"*For you to grow a brain, perhaps?*" Flipping up and over, Rune leveled out, then commenced doing what he excelled at—butting heads with Beauregard. "*I mean, Jesus, Beau... You're French. Don't tell me you've never heard of reconnaissance.*"

Beauregard rolled his eyes. "*We've been reconning for weeks. We've got the bastards in our sights, dead to rights, in the kill zone. Time to—*"

"*We need more information,*" Rune said, glaring at Beauregard.

His friend scoffed. "*More than a month's worth?*"

Rune opened his mouth.

Callas cut off his retort. "*Beau's right. We need to pivot. Reframe the problem. Kill a few Danes, capture Grizgunn, get the Scots' attention, and—*"

"*That's more like it—the Callas we all know and love.*" Beauregard grinned, baring huge fangs. "*Best weapon around is a pissed-off water dragon.*"

Callas huffed in amusement.

Rune laughed. "*We kill some Danes, and Cyprus won't need convincing. The Scots'll come to the table. They'll want to know how Cal found Grizgunn and his merry band of thugs when he and his warriors haven't been able to track 'em.*"

"*That's the idea.*" Filing away details, Callas drew others to the forefront of his mind. "*If we get Grizgunn first, we force Cyprus's hand. I'll make a sit-down with the entire Scottish pack a condition of handing him over. Get to look each warrior in the eye and—*"

"*Determine his origin,*" Rune said.

"Yeah," Callas murmured, excitement spiraling into his low tone.

Finally. Fucking *finally*. A strategy he could get behind.

"I like the new plan," Beauregard said, violence glinting in his pale eyes. *"Much more fun than the old one."*

Rune hummed in agreement.

"More recon first," he said. *"We're outnumbered. We need to figure out how to separate Grizgunn from his pack."*

Beauregard nodded. *"Once we get our claws on him, we'll lock him down and—"*

"Use the asshole as leverage," Callas said, cranking the dial on his tracking beacon. His focus narrowed, enhancing his view of the Danes.

Shrugging his shoulders, Rune flicked rain off his wingtips. *"That's if Cyprus doesn't get his claws on him before we do."*

"Silver dragons. So fucking cerebral," Beauregard said. *"Stop being a killjoy. It's annoying."*

"You didn't say that when I talked those females into—"

With a grin, Beauregard hurled snow at Rune's head.

Horns the color of steel flashed as he ducked. The snowball whistled past. Rune torqued into a sideways flip over Callas's back. Blue eyes gleaming, Beauregard rose to meet him.

The two met with a bang. Sound traveled over the mountaintops.

Focused on the Danes, Callas ignored the scuffle. Nothing but the usual tussle. Dragon warriors at play, fighting for fun, hackles raised, talons up and claws deployed.

Knuckles clanged against scales. Lighthearted growls turned into low snarls. Sliver scales winked in his periphery as Rune spun full circle. His tail whipped around, blurring into a streak. Metallic spikes thumped against white scales.

Beauregard grunted. The temperature dropped. The raindrops traveling in Callas's wake turned to flurries as ice dragon magic sparked, blowing snow everywhere.

Rune nailed Beau again. A crack echoed over the mountain range.

Callas dodged as sheets of ice flew off Beauregard's flank.

"Dirty move, mon ami," Beauregard said. *"Below the belt."*

Rune laughed. *"Buck up, Beau. Stop messing arou—"*

"*Heads up,*" Callas said as Grizgunn changed tack. *"The rogues just pulled a U-turn."*

The squabble ended in an instant.

Aggression replaced it, sucking oxygen out of the air as his brothers-in-arms whirled. Wings spread wide, both warriors settled back into formation. Rune leveled out on Callas's right wingtip. Beauregard set up shop on his left as Callas blasted over a deep gorge. His velocity ripped rock from the mountainside.

Boulders tumbled.

Sound rippled across the valley.

Bending his magic, he silenced the cacophony. As the rumble quieted, he sliced between a tower rock and a steep cliff face. High winds buffeted him. The webbing of his wings stretched. Leaning into the discomfort, he flipped into a sideways somersault, hovered a moment, then set down on the edge of rocky outcropping.

His claws snicked against granite.

Still ten miles from his primary target, Callas settled into a low crouch. His packmates landed alongside him. Wings flapped. Dust swirled. Raindrops fell from his scales, splashing across uneven stone. Ignoring the rivulets, he cranked a magical dial. His vision narrowed. The invisible lens he controlled swiveled, giving him a better view.

Flying over the treetops, sixteen Danes peeled away from the lead dragon, taking up overwatch positions above the valley floor. Two warriors landed in a clearing surrounded by thick woodland.

Gray storm clouds parted.

Moonlight touched down on the valley floor.

Paws on the ground, light blue scales glinting in the glow, Grizgunn shifted from dragon to human form. The male with him followed suit.

Callas angled the lens. Details came into sharper focus. Thick woodland. A river snaking through old-growth trees, and nestled alongside it, an impressive collection of cottages. Small crofts with stone walls, wide windows, and thatched roofs. Dirt roads wound between the houses. Crooked footpaths wandered between pens and chicken coops built to keep livestock in and predators out.

The place looked medieval...and human.

One inhale, and Callas knew better. Humankind didn't live here and never had. The village hidden inside the Grampian Mountains smelled of dark Druids...and stink of black magic.

Dressed in dark robes, Grizgunn strode out of the woods into a ring of standing stones. Ancient Fae in construction, with an altar at its center. Even from this distance, Callas scented the blood that had been spilled inside the sacred circle, some Fae, most of it human.

"Blood sacrifice," Rune snarled. *"Fucked up."*

Unable to disagree, Callas didn't bother to answer. He kept his eyes on Grizgunn, tracking the male's movement as a Druid entered the circle. The two clasped hands. Chairs were brought out. Purple upholstery, plush seat cushions surrounded by wooden high backs and wide, sturdy arms carved with intricate designs.

"*You see 'em?*" Beauregard asked.

Callas nodded.

Folding his wings, Rune glanced at him. "*Audio?*"

"*Tuning in now,*" Callas said, adjusting the antenna on the lens.

Grizgunn and the Druid sat and began talking.

Beauregard nudged Callas with his tail. "*How long we giving it?*"

"*Quiet,*" Rune said. "*Let him listen.*"

"*Five, ten minutes, max.*" Turning a mental dial, Callas searched for the correct frequency.

Radio waves warped inside his mind. A click-click-clicking came through. More fine-tuning. The signal stabilized. High-pitched squawks turned into two distinct voices. Callas tuned into the conversation from a distance, hoping like hell Grizgunn said something he could use.

"*Starting the countdown,*" Beauregard muttered. "*Ten minutes, Cal, then I'm airborne. I need blood on my claws tonight.*"

Callas's mouth curved. Didn't they all?

12

Warnocks thundered down the steep mountain path.

Talons curled around a cliff edge, Levin kept his eyes on the dust cloud in the wake of hammering hooves, tracking the troop's progress—descending straight into the valley, toward the strip of thick woodland set between towering mountain peaks. He scanned the vale, gaze skimming over the forest. A layer of thick fog rolled, rising between the treetops, obscuring the details, though…

He smelled the acrid magic.

"Fae," Tempel murmured, scenting the acidity in the air.

Levin glanced up. *"Ancient."*

Hanging horns down from a hundred feet up, Tempel raised a brow.

Levin drew another deep breath. *"Not a hundred percent Fae, though."*

"Druids."

"A lot of them."

His friend bared a double row of serrated teeth. *"Another clusterfuck. Just like in Savannah. Fae infrastructure overtaken by other Magickind."*

"Aye."

"Makes you wonder what the fucking Fae are doing."

Didn't it, though?

A dominant race, the Fae commanded powerful magic. The kind that could tip the scales and unbalance the world. More than a match for a Dragonkind pack, which made other species speculate and rumors abound. Some said the ancient warrior race hated humankind so much, they'd found a way through the *Ecotone* (the magical veil between worlds), making their home in a parallel universe. Others insisted the Goddess of All Things had wiped them from the face of the earth.

No one knew for sure, but Levin sensed Fae magic everywhere in the valley. From craggy hollows and mountain peaks to the dead leaves littered across the forest floor.

Night vision pinpoint sharp, he leaned over the ledge, trying to get a better read. No dice. The magic-driven shield curving over the valley held tight, resisting his intrusion. No way for him to see through it unless he flew in for a closer look and—

A fist banged on ice. The rapid hammering raged behind him.

"Jesus," Tempel muttered, tone full of amusement.

Shifting his weight from one paw to the other, Levin glanced over his shoulder. With a critical eye, he scanned the outside of the ice shield. Tucked against the mountainside. Hidden deep inside an invisibility spell. Excellent seal against jagged stone. Zero weakness in the outer shell. The perfect place to leave Priya while he investigated the mystery of the valley below.

A sensible solution. The only one that would ensure she stayed safe, well away from the danger, until he returned to take her home.

Not that she agreed with his methods.

On her feet behind the barrier, Priya pounded on the inside of the shield. Only with her left hand, though. The other she kept close, elbow bent, wrist up, plastic cast tucked against her chest.

An image of her crooked fingers rose in his mind's eye.

Fury curled through him. Compassion arrived on its heels. Her discomfort cracked him open, making his heart ache and his mind burn. He wanted to take away her pain. Needed to soothe her so badly, he remained rooted to the cliff—torn between completing the mission and doing right by his mate.

Gaze glued to her blurry silhouette behind the layer of ice, Levin watched her hammer away one-handed. He clenched his teeth. An accident, his arse. Someone had hurt her. Taken a hammer to her knuckles. Smashed her hand while shattering her bones. He knew what torture looked like, along with the effects in the aftermath. Had done that kind of damage to other Dragonkind males, breaking bones, cracking skulls, wreaking physical and emotional havoc during interrogations.

By no means his favorite activity, but he accepted the role, dishing out pain, extracting information to keep his brothers-in-arms safe from enemies, far and wide. Priya, though...

His stomach pitched.

Bile touched the back of his throat.

Goddess help him. He needed to erase the pictures circling inside his head. Images of someone holding her down, making her thrash, forcing screams from her throat while she begged for her life.

A low growl rolled from deep inside his chest.

The bloody bastards. He needed to find out who was responsible. The instant he pulled the information from his mate, he'd fly to London and end their lives. He couldn't live knowing the ones who hurt her still breathed. No matter what kind of trouble she'd found, Priya didn't deserve that kind of treatment.

No female ever did, but—

"Motherfucker!" Getting nowhere with just one fist, Priya kicked the barrier. "I'm going to rip your scales off one by one!"

Tempel snorted.

"Harpoon you through the heart!"

His lips twitched.

"Rip your claws off!"

Enjoying her inventiveness, Levin shook his head, then conjured a fluffy blanket and tossed it over the back of chaise-longue. Voice muffled, she yelled another threat. Watching her stamp her feet, he added more books to the pile and another box of biscuits—lemon-cream shortbread to complement the chocolate ones already sitting beside the ice chair.

Her head snapped toward the gifts.

Tapped into her bio-energy, he felt her temper flare brighter. A little growl sounded next. Stomping toward the chair, she kicked one of the boxes. The cardboard carton went airborne. As it smashed on stone, the top exploded open, sending lemon-cream-filled treats flying across the alcove. Unable to help himself, he smiled. It wasn't funny. Nothing about the situation was laughable, but...Goddess. She was adorable, in such a froth she forgot to be afraid.

An excellent sign.

The events in her past hadn't damaged her spirit. At least, not overmuch. Less than an hour after meeting him, she'd stepped away from fear, allowing her true colors to shine through. Awe filled him as he watched her, her beauty so blinding he lost himself for a moment, seeing nothing but her.

The urge to connect streamed through him.

He should leave her be, allow her to settle, keep his position beyond the alcove a secret from her, but need was a tricky beast, and the temptation too great. He wanted the connection, craved a taste, longed to see her bio-energy flare when she heard his voice. Before he took to the sky and left her behind.

Reaching out with his mind, Levin touched hers. *"Priya, lass—calm down. Ye're safe. Pick up a book, eat a biscuit, and—"*

"Forget about the harpoon. I'm going boil you in acid," she said, aura filling out, intense bio-energy burning bright around her.

Enthralled by the light show, he felt satisfaction surge through him.

"You've got yourself a spitfire, Lev," Tempel said, laughter coming through mind-speak. *"She's pissed."*

"As long as she's safe, my mate can be as angry as she wants."

"Wise, though...wouldn't wanna be you later."

"Bullshite. You absolutely would."

"Fucking right," Tempel mumbled. *"I'd give anything to meet my mate."*

Most Dragonkind males would.

The reaction made his friend normal. And now, after touching Priya, Levin understood why.

Everything about her enlivened him. Without even trying, she drew him deeper with every exchange, making him wish they'd met under different circumstances. Better ones more conducive to courting a female. Given half a chance, he would've made the effort, put in the time, wooed her right, ensuring her transition into his world was an easy one.

Fate, however, had intervened, sending her to him at an unexpected time in an unexpected place. Something to be thankful for, no matter how messed up it was right now.

Sensation swept along his spine. The tips of his horns started to tingle.

Head swiveling, green gaze aglow, Tempel looked south. *"The boys."*

"Twelve miles out." Sonar pinging, Levin tracked his

packmates' progress. Playing catch and receive, he broadcast his location. With a quick shift, Cyprus and the others changed tack, slicing across the night sky to meet him. *"Get airborne."*

Ripping rocks from the mountain, Tempel left his perch.

As shale tumbled, Levin dragged his gaze from Priya. His muscles coiled, making his scales click as he leapt up, pushed out, twisting into a spine-torquing somersault. Damp air whistled over his horns. The rocky snarl at the base of the cliff rose to meet him. Letting go of the tuck, he opened his wings. An updraft caught in the webbing, catapulting him into the sky. Spikes rattling, aggression rising, he banked hard, blasting around the mountainside.

Ahead of him, Tempel sliced between two rock formations.

Static hissed between Levin's temples.

Cyprus's voice streamed into his head. *"Details, Lev."*

"Warnocks entering a valley. Bound by Fae magic. No visibility," Levin said, checking his distance to target. His eyes narrowed. Seven miles until he pierced the magical shield. *"Trace energy everywhere. Smells like Fae, feels like Druids."*

"Legion," Tempel growled, scenting what Levin did on the wind.

Rannock growled. *"Outstanding."*

"About fucking time," Vyroth said.

"Fighting triangles?" Fire dragon raging, the sound of an inferno hissed through the link as Tydrin asked, *"Or are we going two by two?"*

"Pairs," Wallaig said, deep voice little more than a snarl. *"North, south, east, and west. I want the bastards surrounded."*

"No escape? Or are we taking prisoners?" Kruger asked, taking the pack's temperature.

A good call. Violent by nature, the male would annihilate everything in his path without clarification.

"*Kill only those who resist. Round up the rest,*" Cyprus said, voice firm. "*We need tae know if any more encampments exist. I want the exact locations. Nothing left tae chance, lads. We end it here, tonight, even if it means—*"

"*Fuck,*" Kruger growled. "*We've got warriors in the weeds.*"

Unable to see past the Fae shield, Levin asked, "*Druid or Dragonkind?*"

Mind-speak warped as Kruger recalibrated. "*Dragonkind. All over the fucking place.*"

A glint of excitement in his eyes, Tempel threw him a sideways glance. "*About time we flew into something fun.*"

Narrowing his focus, Levin frowned. Nothing on his radar, no unique energy signals coming from enemy warriors in the air. Though that didn't mean his packmate was wrong.

A freak of nature, Kruger blurred the lines between Dragonkind subsets. Sometimes, the male embraced his Metallic side. Other times, he pulled out venomous, fire, and earth dragon skills. Wallaig called Kruger's magic majestic. Levin labeled it fantastic. Especially when his friend latched on to a pack's unique signature, tracking the enemy from vast distances.

A wonder when it worked. Frustrating as hell for Kruger when the rogues disappeared before he locked on.

"*I need numbers, Kruger.*" Speed supersonic, Levin rocketed over the top of a spiked ridgeline. "*How many we looking at?*"

"*I cannae tell yet. I'm still too far away, but I've got multiple signals,*" Kruger said, deep voice cutting through mind-speak like a buzzsaw. "*I sense three males, ten miles tae the north. More perched along the mountain range. Cloaked. Hidden. Above the valley floor.*"

"*Kruger,*" Cyprus said. "*Ye're on point. Fly in under the radar. I wanna know what we're dealing with before we break through the three-mile marker."*

Kruger hummed, the low sound full of anticipation. *"Levin—"*

"Coming around now. Tempel—break off. Join the others." Tilting his wings, Levin changed his trajectory. A faint ping sounded inside his head. Eyes on the sky, he expanded the cloaking spell, pushing it out until it merged with Kruger's. Emerald-green scales with blood-red accents came into view. He hit the brakes, shifting into a smooth glide behind his packmate. The rough edges of his magic smoothed out. One blink, and Levin dropped off radar, becoming invisible to others of his kind. *"On yer six, brother."*

"Stay in my draft, Lev."

"I'm already in the stream."

With a flick of his tail, Kruger slowed his wing speed. The voltage around him amplified. Thin threads of electricity arced into the air. Static electricity zipped over Levin's scales. Shrugging off the tingles, he unleashed his magic. The temperature dropped. Frost rolled like fog inside the cloaking spell, throwing a blanket over the magical burn, keeping his packmate's wattage below the threshold of detection.

The entire reason Kruger wanted him on his tail. Levin's ice killed almost anything. Once engaged, nothing broke through his frost shield. The output from Kruger's high-powered magic included. Without him, the male might be able to stay under enemy radar. Good odds, but not perfect ones. A fifty-fifty chance at best. His frost, however, increased the odds, turning an iffy covert mission into a successful one.

"Two o'clock," Levin murmured. *"Three males, fighting triangle, perched close to the peak on the right."*

"Another trio on the left, across the valley," Kruger muttered back, flying a zigzag pattern across the sky, continuing his sweep. *"More warriors hiding upwind."*

"Flankers."

"Four..." His horns tilted as he paused. *"Nay, five groups plus one. Sixteen warriors total."*

"And the males to the north?"

"Stationary. Holding steady ten miles out."

"You getting a read?"

Kruger shook his head, then glanced over his shoulder. Black eyes glittering with the promise of violence, he met Levin's gaze. *"Wanna shake the tree?"*

"See who falls out?" Levin grinned. *"My money's on Grizgunn."*

"What's he doing meeting with Druids?"

"Donnae know, but I wanna find out."

Kruger tipped his chin. *"Moving west. I want the high ground."*

"Agreed." One by one, Levin marked each of the rogues' positions, dropping pins onto a mental map. A number of warriors hung in deep crevices. Others gathered in the gloom along narrow ledges cut into the mountainside. The last three choose rocky terrain, looking more like boulders than dragons, sitting close to the valley floor. As the last pin landed, Levin pushed the information through to the rest of the pack. *"Countdown is on, lads. Wait for my signal."*

His brothers-in-arms growled in agreement.

Frost flowing over his scales, Levin banked into a tight turn. Four miles to the Fae shield covering the valley floor. Within striking distance of the Danish pack. Soon, he would have what he wanted. What he'd been working toward and hoping for the last few months—the enemy in his sights, and (if he got lucky) Grizgunn's blood on his claws.

13

Grizgunn didn't trust the male sitting across from him.

The chairs, though, were fucking nice.

The purple upholstery made him feel regal. The gold gilding on the arms and headrest appeased his love of pageantry. Thick-cushioned, thronelike, so comfortable he wondered how the Druid would react if he took the pair with him when he got up and left.

Owning the matched set would be sweet. Planting the armchairs in his bedroom, where he saw them every day when he woke, would be even better. Conquest, after all, needed to be not only celebrated, but put on display.

Not that the Druid knew he was in trouble yet.

Tamarack thought he was gaining an ally in his war against innkeeper at The White Hare. The Druid wanted Ferguson McGilvery dead. Grizgunn didn't care one way or the other, but since he'd always enjoyed a good revenge story, he waited the male out, eager to hear the plan.

A breeze blew into the sacred circle of standing stones, ruffling the hair curling over the nape of his neck. Black gaze on his, Tamarack settled deeper into his chair. Nonchalant. Confident. Leaning into the silence as Grizgunn did the same. Bent elbows to the armrest, he laced his fingers, then set the side of his boot on top of his knee.

Quiet swelled.

Gaze steady on Tamarack, he didn't bother breaking it. He absorbed the silence instead, reveling in the tension. The Druid shifted in his seat, giving away his discomfort.

Grizgunn's mouth curved.

Not so puffed up with self-importance now, was he? On home turf, surrounded by his Druid brothers and sisters (and substantial amounts of Fae magic), the male believed he couldn't touch him. A bad assumption, and sitting in the presence of a Dragonkind commander, Tamarack changed his mind. Grizgunn saw the mental shift happen as self-assurance gave way to uncertainty, chipping at the male's confidence.

Grizgunn bit back a sigh. He'd expected more from the leader of Legion.

How much more?

He pursed his lips. At a bare minimum, the male—a savant touted by Druids all over the British Isles—should've done his homework. Dug a little deeper. Unearthed a lot more. Any leader with half a brain would've said no to the sit-down with a member of the Dragonkind elite. Done the research. Made some calls and discovered Grizgunn never played well with others.

He dominated. He harassed. He used subterfuge, making his mark believe one thing while he made something else happen.

All part of the game. One he enjoyed playing. Tonight, especially, given what he had to gain—an edge. The sliver of supremacy he needed to force Cyprus and the Scottish pack's hand.

The swish of long robes rushed over fresh-cut grass.

Three handmaidens walked single file between massive standing stones. The trio didn't look at him. Nor did they say a word. Moving with purpose, one set a small table on the ground between him and Tamarack. The second set down a pair of teacups complete with fancy-ass saucers. The last arrived carrying an ornate pot. Each movement graceful, she poured.

Steam curled up from the surface of the dark brew.

Head bowed, eyes lowered, she passed him his cup.

Fine china rattled in its saucer.

Shifting forward in his seat, Grizgunn took what was offered. His fingers brushed hers in the exchange. The muscles roping his abdomen tightened. His gaze roamed her face. Not bad. Earthy scent, exquisite features. Not a high-energy female, but not a low one either. Somewhere in between, the blonde was arresting, deserving of his time and attention, and—

"You like what you see?" Tamarack asked.

Grizgunn raised a brow. "Was that your intention? To distract me with pretty handmaidens?"

The male smiled. "The thought had occurred."

"Are you offering her services?"

The blonde tensed beside the table. Alarm flared in her bio-energy, the green, pink, and gold of her aura as pretty as her face. Gaze glued to the leader of Legion, Grizgunn drank in the spark, his dragon half becoming impatient and restless.

Tamarack shrugged. "Perhaps. Afterward. If we reach an equitable agreement."

Grizgunn leaned back in his chair. "Equitable to me might not be the same for you."

"You would be wise to take me seriously, dragon," he murmured, a hint of threat underpinning his tone. "I've salted the earth with the corpses of those who have underestimated me."

"Well then..." Pleased by the show of strength, Grizgunn raised his tea in salute. "I do believe we'll get along just fine."

With a smile that never reached his eyes, the Druid returned the gesture, then flicked his free hand. The handmaidens turned and left the same way they arrived. Without uttering a word. Walking in single file. Robes swished around their bare feet, disappearing into the gloom.

"What do you hope to gain with this alliance?" Raising the ridiculous teacup, Tamarack took a sip. "You haven't paid The White Hare any attention...until now."

"Leverage."

"Against the Scottish pack."

Grizgunn nodded. "We have similar goals, you and me. You want control of The White Hare. I want the innkeeper."

Dark eyes leveled on him, Tamarack quirked a brow. "Why? What good will the innkeeper do you?"

"You help me capture her—"

"You command a dragon horde, Grizgunn—capture her yourself."

"I can't enter the grounds of The White Hare," he said, the admission tasting like poison in his mouth. Swallowing the dry burn, he gentled his grip on the cup before it shattered in his hand. "I've tried more than once, but the Parkland refuses me and my warriors entry every time. But you...your tribe comes and goes without issue."

"Ah," Tamarack said, understanding lighting his eyes.

"Why is that?"

"One of my kin fucked a Fae warrior. Surprise pregnancy with unintended consequences. Ancient history, five generations ago, but—"

"You still reap the benefits."

Teacup resting on his thigh, Tamarack inclined his

head. "It's enough to fool the spirit of the Parkland, allowing me to slip over her borders, into the innkeeper's territory."

"Sneak attacks."

"Only way to kill her."

Holding his cup by its saucer, Grizgunn fought the urge to hurl the stupid thing against one of the standing stones. Losing his temper wouldn't aid his cause. No matter how much he hated tea, he needed to stay on track. Focus was key. Getting sidetracked by a pointless ritual—the chairs, he understood. Foul-tasting tea served by beautiful females, he did not—wouldn't move the agenda forward.

So instead so spitting it out, he forced himself to take another sip. Swallowing the awful brew, he smoothed his expression to avoid insulting his host. The custom might be idiotic, but until the Druid agreed, he must stay on message...and show a little respect.

"We can help each other, Tamarack."

"What makes you think I need your help?" Leaning forward, the Druid set the cup on the table. He picked up the pot, poured himself more, then resettled in his chair. "I'm—"

"Nowhere."

Dark eyes blacker than pitch met Grizgunn's.

He met the challenge head-on, refusing to look away. "You're not any closer to your goal than I am."

"I want The White Hare. Non-negotiable."

Well, all right then. Finally. He was getting somewhere.

Grizgunn shrugged. "The inn along with the land is yours as long I get the innkeeper."

"Why do you want her?"

"Why do you care?"

"I want her dead, dragon, not banging around Scotland. Her magic is at its peak inside the Parkland. If she's alive, I risk the chance of her coming back. Once I control the Parkland and the powerful magic it wields, it stays with me and my tribe. As it should have remained from the beginning. Legion will not risk having it wrested from our control by a—"

"And if I assure you she won't live long once I have her?"

Tamarack paused with the cup halfway to his mouth. "You'll have to get past her mate. I've seen the bastard. Kruger's powerful, the entire reason we haven't been to get close to her after our first attempt on her life."

The explosion inside the innkeeper's private quarters.

Grizgunn had heard about it. The intel, along with the information Tigmar (his pack's IT specialist) dug up, was the reason he'd wanted to meet with Tamarack tonight. He didn't like Druids or Fae, but the old idiom remained true—the enemy of my enemy is my friend. Alone, neither his pack or the tribe held the power to oust the Scottish pack. Together, however, they could accomplish the annihilation of a mutual enemy.

Staring at him, Tamarack tilted his head. "How do you envision it playing out?"

"You get me into the Parkland…under the wire, undetected." Taking his ankle from his knee, Grizgunn abandoned his tea on the table. Setting his forearms on his thighs, he leaned forward. "Once I'm there, I'll be cloaked, invisible to other Magickind…able to move freely through The White Hare."

"Won't work. Kruger will see you coming from miles away."

"Only if he's on the grounds."

"A distraction."

"One big enough to draw the entire Scottish pack far from the Parkland."

"Snatch and grab."

"Exactly," Grizgunn said. "Once I have her, you'll be free to move in and take control."

"Seems too easy."

"The best plans often are," he murmured, his attention rapt on the Druid.

Intelligence alive in his eyes, Tamarack drummed his fingers against the arm of his chair. The rapid tap echoed. The paused lengthened. One beat turned into two before the male shrugged. "Worth a try."

Triumph settled deep. A spark of excitement followed. "Then we have an accord."

Tamarack tipped his chin. "We do, dragon."

"Good." Pushing to his feet, Grizgunn gave his new ally a set of coordinates. The place he wanted the leader of Legion to meet him. A deserted spot he'd reconned on the western edge of the Parkland. "Three days, Druid."

"Seventy-two hours." Pulling a pocket watch from his pocket, Tamarack flipped it open and marked the time. "I'll be there."

With nothing left to discuss, Grizgunn tipped his chin and walked away. Past the bloodstained altar. Between two standing stones. Becoming one with the darkness, he reengaged his sonar. A buzz went off inside his head as he strode toward the riverbank. Moonlight and Fae magic combined, painting a path through the forest, gilding thick branches and full canopies with silver light.

Old leaves crunched beneath his boot treads. The smell of rushing water came to him. Moving around a scarred tree trunk, he skirted a grouping of croft houses. All quiet. No Druids milling around outside. Though he could hear the low murmur of voices farther upstream, close to the base of the cliffs. Night vision pinpoint sharp, he looked that way. Steam twisted up from beyond the tree line, rising from hot springs chiseled into the rock.

A well-organized encampment protected by dense woodland. One nestled in a deep valley surrounded by mountains on all sides. Nice setup. The Druids had chosen their base of operations well.

Delight took a trip down his spine, making him shiver.

After he captured the innkeeper, the Druid lands and homesteads would be next. Having a refuge deep in the Grampians—a place to lie low if his warrior couldn't make it back to home base—would be an excellent addition to the real estate portfolio he was building inside Scottish territory.

Hakon, his second-in-command, materialized out of the shadows.

Grizgunn met his gaze. "You heard?"

His friend nodded.

"All of it?"

"Yeah, though noticed you left out a few details," Hakon said, humor infusing his voice.

"Tamarack doesn't need to know the whole of it."

Vicious by nature, sadistic by choice, Hakon smiled.

Grizgunn returned it and—

His sonar pinged.

Static washed into his head.

Powered by Fae magic, the shield protecting Tamarack's territory vibrated like a tuning fork. Interference hissed through the connection, twisting the signal until it blurred.

The warning jackhammered through him.

With a curse, Grizgunn reached out to his pack. Radio silence. A dead signal instead of quick responses from his warriors through mind-speak.

Cut off from his pack, Grizgunn growled, "Incoming."

"A shit-ton, by the sounds of it." Yellow eyes glowing like twin spot lights, Hakon glanced around the woods.

"From every direction. You got anything? A signal? Comms?"

Head tilted back, Grizgunn stared up through the treetops. Stormy sky. Fast-moving clouds. Fae magic warping into multicolored waves. "Nothing."

"We're fucked."

No need to state the obvious. That about summed it up.

"We need to get airborne."

"Go," Hakon growled, taking off through the trees.

Boot soles digging into dead leaves and soft soil, Grizgunn raced after his warrior. Dodging trees, cutting around boulders, he sprinted toward for the dell where he'd landed earlier. He needed to reach the edge of the woods, enter the clearing, and get airborne. Once he flew past the shield and gained enough altitude, he'd acquire the signal and activate his warriors.

Sending out the call was imperative.

His pack needed to be warned now, before whoever had broken through the three-mile marker figured out he was still on the ground and took advantage of his position.

A dragon stuck on the ground, after all, always ended up dead.

14

Coming up like a shark from below, Levin climbed between two rockfaces. His claws found small nooks, clicking over the cliff face. Sound warped inside the invisibility spell, protecting him from detection. Frost fogged every breath. He didn't notice. Didn't clear the icy swirl or adjust his position.

His focus stayed on the Dane.

Killing the male was a formality. Already done, even though the idiot still breathing didn't know it yet.

Disappointment buzzed through him. Like a chainsaw being cranked, his conscience roared to life, cutting through the blur of aggression. The takedown would be too easy. He frowned. What in the fuck was the bastard thinking? The Dane should know better than to hang upside down inside a crevice—one of the most obvious hidey-holes on the mountainside.

His gaze narrowed on the rogue's scaly black hide. What to do...what to do? Give the bastard a sporting chance? Or slice him in two without warning?

Levin debated a moment.

Wind howled through the narrow ravine. Dust kicked up. Stones blew off the ledge above his head. Shale rained down. Rock pinged against rock, then bounced off his cloaking spell without making a sound.

Two separate, very different sounds—one hard, the other soft. Levin froze, waiting for the Dane to grow a brain and catch on.

He waited. And waited…and waited some more.

Nothing. Hanging in midair, gaze trained on the valley floor like an automaton waiting for someone to flip his switch, the Dane didn't twitch.

Levin sighed. Well, guess that answered *that*. In his world, brutality ruled. Which meant no one this inept deserved to keep his life…and Levin was seconds away from getting blood on his claws.

Anticipation burned through him. His heart thumped hard as his muscles quickened.

Clenching his teeth, Levin bit back a snarl and continued to climb. Thirty feet away. Now fifteen. Rooted to the underside of an outcropping, he leapt from one cliff face to the other. His angle of attack improved.

Tail curled over his spine like a scorpion, he moved like a sidewinder across jagged rock and opened a channel into mind-speak. *"In position."*

"Thirty seconds," Kruger said as stormy skies rumbled above him. *"Got three in the pipe. Wait for me. We strike together."*

"Cy," Levin murmured, checking on the rest of the pack.

"All set." Falling like dominoes, the click of scales came through the link. Wings flapped. A low growl sounded as his commander settled into his chosen perch. *"Multiple males in the kill zone. You call it, we go."*

Levin nodded even though no one could see him. *"Rannock—"*

"In the boulders on the edge of the valley floor. Got Tempel with me," his friend said, liquid metal bubbling at the back of his throat, causing his voice to roughen. An excellent sign. As a bronze dragon, Rannock embraced his Metallic side, running toward savagery at full speed. *"Anyone tries tae fly out of there, we'll get him."*

"Capture and carry, Ran," Cyprus said, reminding everyone of the objective. *"I want a couple Danes tae interrogate. We need tae know where Grizgunn and his inner circle sleeps."*

Rannock grumbled his displeasure.

"Seriously? I don't get to kill anyone?" Tempel asked. *"I don't want to be Rannock's wing-mate anymore. Someone trade with me."*

Wallaig laughed.

"No way," Tydrin and Vyroth said at the same time.

"Suck it up, Yankee Doodle," Rannock growled, sounding as pissed off as Tempel. *"We're in perfect position. No backing out now."*

Tempel mumbled something obscene.

Poised to strike, Levin brushed aside the byplay. *"Sound off, lads."*

His brothers-in-arms chimed in one after another. As he listened to each male settle into position and give him the green light, he tracked Kruger's progress across the mountain range. Half a mile to the north. Far enough to strike a different trio of Danes, close enough to fly in and provide cover if Levin needed it.

The last to answer, Kruger said, *"Good tae—"*

"Go," Levin snarled.

With a push, he propelled himself upward. He grabbed the Dane's tail. Sharp spikes bit into his palm. His claws found the soft spot between black scales. The hooked tips bit, slicing through flesh to meet bone. With a startled howl, the male swung his head around. Wide yellow eyes full of shock met his a second before Levin yanked the male out of the narrow crevice.

Blood rushed over his talons.

Another hard jerk. Another scream of pain as the bottom dropped out. In free fall toward the bottom of the ravine, Levin climbed the enemy dragon's spine like a tree. Tearing through his scales. Slashing at his wings.

Leaving deep wounds as he reached for the bastard's horns.

Talons scrambling against stone, the rogue twisted in his grasp, jamming his wingtips into the parallel vertical faces.

His backward slide stopped.

With a growl, Levin deployed his back paws and grabbed the male's tail. He wrenched. Heavy vertebrae snapped. Interlocking dragon skin ripped loose. Arterial spray spurted across his chest, bathing his pale tiger-striped scales red. Showing no mercy, he conjured his ice daggers. Twin blades working in tandem, he cut flesh from bone, filleting the male like a fish.

Gravity took hold. The Dane started to fall.

Levin grabbed the bastard by the horns. A quick twist, and bones snapped. Opening the cloaking spell, he allowed sound to escape. The brutal crack ricocheted, echoing over the ridgeline like a warning shot.

The Dane's heart stopped beating as he fell. The black dragon disintegrated, bursting into a flurry of ash before hitting the jagged rocks below. Gray flakes exploded up the crevice, coating his scales as Levin tucked his wings. Arching backward, he flipped into a somersault. His tail whiplashed. Sharp spikes cut across granite. The shriek roared between cliffs as he plummeted, revolving into a downward spiral.

Rock dust and dragon ash blew into his face.

Seconds before he face-planted into the rocks, he opened his wings. White webbing stretched. Wind rush lifted his bulk, slingshotting him into the sky. Thunder rumbled. Distant lightning flashed across the valley, scoring across jagged peaks and dark green forest.

Tingles ghosted over his horns as his sonar pinged.

His attention snapped toward the western range. Trace energy everywhere. Adjusting his radar, he hunted for the enemy in open skies. Six unique energy signatures, flying in tight formation. Two trios of dragon warriors heading his way.

His mouth curved.

Banking hard, Levin moved to intercept. He increased his velocity. A sonic boom sounded as he broke the sound barrier. Ice chips whistled from his tail. Frost chased him across the sky as eagerness flooded his veins. A natural reaction, given the oncoming fight, and the satisfaction of a good kill. Though—he bared his fangs—Dane number one hadn't been what he expected.

After going months without a proper fight, he'd wanted experience. A good two-way brawl. What he'd gotten instead was an untrained warrior. One who hadn't been able to hide, never mind find a way to use his claws. Which raised a question...

What the hell had Grizgunn been doing since he arrived in Scotland?

Not training his warriors, that was for certain.

Months and months lost while Levin searched for the Danes. Days and weeks spent working his contacts, talking to his CIs in hopes of locating the rogue pack. All that time and effort felt like a waste, given the intel that never brought results. The Danish pack had stayed hidden, flying beneath the radar until now.

A responsible Dragonkind commander would've used that time wisely. Spent every night schooling the warriors in the ways of close-quarter claw-to-claw tactics, along with every other aspect of dragon combat training.

It wasn't rocket science.

Winning battles took practice. Teaching warriors how to fight together required repetition—a lot of it, in the sky and on the ground. But more than anything, a Dragonkind pack needed a strong leader. A male who would fight and die for those he commanded.

The dragon warrior he'd killed hadn't been prepared.

Which meant Grizgunn sucked at his job.

The realization cranked Levin tight, which pissed him off. He should be celebrating the first kill of the night, calling out to his pack to relay the good news—and tweak his packmates' tails. Competition and camaraderie, after all, never went out of style. His packmates loved to hear the details, then discuss tactics, hard targets, and shared goals.

But as Levin blasted across the sky in search of another fight, he didn't feel like celebrating. KO'ing the male had been too easy. A hollow victory turned complete letdown. Nothing to savor about the kill. No highlights to share when he and his packmates arrived back at the lair. Little more than the hiccup of his heartbeat—along with the realization that, so far, the rogues weren't just interlopers squatting in territory ruled by the Scottish pack. The Danes were also idiots who possessed few skills and absolutely no backbone.

Disheartening, to say the least.

After dreaming about clashing with the enemy for months, he'd hoped for better. More smarts. More speed. A more spirited fight (not near capitulation) when he got his claws on one. Just a little something special—pure aggression, some extra spice, combined with the guts to use it.

Was that really too much to ask?

Was he doomed to—

A snarl blasted through mind-speak. *"Levin—move the fuck out of my way."*

Sensing his friend behind him, Levin torqued into a spine-bending flip. Emerald and red scales nothing but a blur, Kruger rocketed underneath him. At the height of his spin, Levin heard a low growl and—

Claws clanged against scales.

Powerful magic whiplashed. A metallic green glow suffused the air.

A rogue yelped.

Frost streaming off his wingtips, Levin whipped upright. His night vision sparked and sharpened. Tilting his wings, he roared into a tight turn as Kruger grabbed one rogue by the throat and stabbed another one with his tail.

Scales cracked. Screams echoed. Dragon ash exploded into the air.

Entering the fray, Levin lashed out. His claw bit. He yanked, ripping a hole in the red dragon's wing. The male tipped sideways and lashed out. He ducked. The paw swung wide. Levin came back up and let fly. His knuckles slammed into the side of the male's skull. The Dane's head whiplashed. Fangs bared, Levin hit him again, and again, then reached up, grabbed hold, and ripped the bastard's horns off.

As he squawked, Levin put the sharp tool to use, killing the Dane with his own horns.

"Heads up." Opening his talons, Kruger dropped the lime-green dragon.

The rogue ashed out.

Levin's radar squawked. Flicking ash from between his talons, he changed tack. *"Six males flying. Half a mile out. I'm taking first blood."*

Kruger grinned. *"Only if you get there first."*

"Glutton." Curving one wing under, Levin rocketed out of a turn. Magic burned through his veins. Ice exploded behind him, propelling him across the sky like a jet engine.

Wind screamed off his scales. A storm kicked up, blowing his friend off course.

Choking on a face full of snow, Kruger cursed. *"Fuck you. That's cheating."*

"All's fair," he muttered, calculating the distance to target.

"*Divide and conquer,*" Kruger said, trying to keep up. "*Which three do you want?*"

Levin glanced at this friend. "*The first three or four are mine. You get the leftovers.*"

"*You suck.*"

"*Stay focused,*" he growled as the lead rogue came into view.

Big male. Red and yellow scales. Fire dragon vibes and—

The rogue opened his mouth and exhaled. Fire exploded from his throat. Flames streaked across the sky, powering through the darkness. The stench of burned plastic and gasoline obliterated the fresh air.

"*Shite,*" Kruger said. "*Shut it down, Lev.*"

Conjuring his ice, Levin closed the gap, going nose to nose with the inferno. Heat wafted into his face. He counted off the seconds. Fifty yards from being incinerated, he threw up a wall of ice, seven feet thick. Harder than stone. Much more effective as the fireball slammed into the barrier. Ice shards mixed with water exploded up and out, punching a hole through the clouds.

Ice conquered fire.

Yellow and red flames winked out.

The wall folded inward.

With a murmur, Levin crumpled the remaining ice into a ball. Grabbing it on the flyby, he hurled it sidearm at the rogues. Kruger laughed. The Danes slammed on the brakes, then dove sideways, scrambling to get out of the way. Not fast enough, the last warrior in line caught the ice ball with his face.

Bone cracked. Dragon teeth flew. More ash puffed into the air.

"*Bowling for rogues. I like it,*" Kruger murmured, splitting wide right to avoid getting hit with blood spatter. "*Fucking fun.*"

Ignoring his friend, Levin unleashed another round

of daggers. One after one, ice left his palms like automatic gunfire. Knives sliced through scales. A cacophony of curses ripped through the air. Following the deadly spray, he hammered the lead male. The bastard's head whiplashed. Ripped from his hide, red and yellow scales spun across the sky, flying like Chiclets flicked from a box.

A pop sounded.

Smoke rose from the bastard's throat.

Levin hit him again. Claws slashing, ice daggers flying, he kept the other rogues at bay while he adjusted his grip. Talon wrapped around the red dragon wings, he bent both back and whipped full circle. One revolution turned into two. At the height of the spin, he hurled the rogue at his wing-mates.

The trio dodged.

Dark blue scales glimmering, the bigger male dove to save his friend from slamming into the boulders below. The other two turned tail, flying away so fast interlocking dragon skin left yellow and green streaks in their wake.

"*Fuck*," Levin growled.

"*Go after 'em*," Kruger said, cracking skulls on his side of the fight. "*I'll finish up here and—*"

Snap, crackle…

Boom!

As the detonation rippled, Levin's attention snapped to his right. He saw the vortex open. Five Danes flew out of its mouth. Cyprus gave chase, fire acid streaming over his black, white-speckled scales, orange wings blazing a trail across the night sky. Right on his blood brother's tail, Tydrin exited the wormhole, fire dragon on point, dark purple dragon skin ablaze with blue and orange flames.

Pale violet eyes glowing, Cyprus snarled at Levin. "*Grab those two, Lev. Try tae keep at least one of the arseholes alive. We'll finish up here.*"

"Copy that." Whipping around, Levin searched the sky for the rogues who got away.

He found the duo on his second sweep, flying fast, headed toward the Grampians framing the eastern side of the valley—on a collision course with the outcropping, about to flight overtop of the place he left Priya.

Panic cut through him. *"Fucking hell."*

Dragging a rogue backward through the air, Tydrin growled, *"What's wrong?"*

"My female."

A pause in the action. Battle sounds died down for a second, then—

"Who?" Cyprus asked, sounding incredulous.

"Priya. I left her on a ledge and... Shite." Levin's stomach clenched as concern struck. *"She was pissed off. Energy flaming all over the place. If the rogues get too close—"*

Cyprus cursed. *"Go."*

Levin didn't hesitate.

Maxing out his magic, he blasted after the pair. Nothing mattered now but reaching his mate. The shield he'd conjured to keep her safe wasn't foolproof. Magic faded with distance. Without him close, ice always melted. And sometimes cloaking spells cracked... especially with the volatile energy of an HE female involved.

15

Dodging around the side of a bluff, Grizgunn sprinted toward the tree line. Chest pumping, breaths rasping against the back of his throat, he zipped between two trunks. The terrain dipped. Shifting his weight to his heels, he leapt over a log without slowing down. Dead leaves crunched underfoot. Tree limbs swayed overhead as Dragonkind magic clashed with ancient Fae.

Damp air warmed. Mist gathered along the ground a second before bright color danced through the forest. Pinpricks of shimmering pink moved from green to gold, then shifted into blue, creating visual interference.

Clenching his teeth, he sliced through the mystical wave. Electric current crackled over his skin. Sound warped inside his head. His sonar malfunctioned, muffling the signal, inhibiting his ability to see the battle being fought in the sky above him.

A problem he couldn't solve until he got airborne.

The preternatural shield protecting the valley blocked every message he sent. The ping-pong of mental energy made his head hurt. He stayed with it anyway, fighting to remain focused, sending out instructions, hoping one of his pack would hear him and respond.

Silence met his efforts. No one answered. Not a single word came back through the link. Every frequency he tried failed, driving frustration into his soul.

He wasn't worried about the original members of his pack.

Hakon and the others knew how to fight. He and his warriors had perfected the art of hiding in the mountains, too. A necessary skill, given the Scottish pack's dogged pursuit of him. If the fighting become too intense, his personal guard would retreat to the rendezvous point and await further instructions.

The recent additions to his pack, however?

Grizgunn cursed under his breath. The warriors he was in the process of training needed a lot of work. Rejected by the Archguard in Prague, the males had come from all over, responding to the invitation he'd posted on a forum buried deep in the dark net, an online haven for rogue Dragonkind. Though he should've been more specific in his post.

He'd wanted experienced warriors. He'd received a bunch of younglings instead. Males ill-equipped to tangle with warriors of the Scottish pack's caliber.

Cunning and vicious, Cyprus had proven a worthy opponent.

His pact with Tamarack, however, had the potential to tip the scales in his favor. He might not like working with Legion, but after weeks of toying with Cyprus, something needed to give. Besting the Scots meant being bold by pushing boundaries. Which put him here, in a valley powered by ancient Fae, now control by Druids, while males who weren't ready clashed with a vicious pack of killers...right above his fucking head.

Heart pounding, Grizgunn raced down a steep slope. The ground fell away at the bottom. With a grunt, he jumped over the jagged crag onto the dirt trail below. His knees rebounded into his chest, knocking the breath from his lungs. Tall trees gave way to a wild row of hedges. Without slowing, he leapt over the five-foot barrier.

The clearing opened up in front of him.

Each breath rasping in his lungs, he planted his foot on top of a boulder and leapt skyward. Instinct and magic collided as his dragon half took over. Raw power catapulted him into the air. The forest groaned. Fae magic went dark. Undulating color faded as treetops whiplashed and—

Presto, change-o.

His bones lengthened under the fall of light blue scales. Hands and feet turning to talons with hooked claws, he bared his fangs, reveling in the release as huge horns punched through the top of his skull.

True to his skull dragon roots, his horns were three times the average size, curling up like a ram's, rolling over to coil against the sides of his head. An unusual feature for a Dragonkind warrior. His cross to bear. He'd heard the laughter after his *first shift*, suffered through the nasty comments. Endured the whispering and pointing at dragon combat school. The experience made him stronger, tougher…much more brutal. Now, he no longer cared what other males thought when he showed up in dragon form.

What others thought didn't matter. No one but those closest to him needed to know the ins and outs of his magic.

And as radio waves warped, he counted his blessings and, with a murmur, put his unusual gift to good use. Sensation knocked on his skull. His horns vibrated. The size of pinpricks, tiny holes opened along rough ridges scored into solid bone. Shuffling through mental index cards, Grizgunn picked his poison and turned the valve. Hallucinogenic gas leaked from the perforations, trailing over his spine into open air as he gained more altitude.

Released by the gas, a song began to play.

A little extreme, given he didn't know what awaited him above the shield, but…

Messing with a male's mind, lulling him into a slow death with a poison song, always improved his mood. Great upside to being a skull dragon. The downside, though, made him think hard before he unleashed a song. Generating the music-filled gas drained his energy, weakening him in the aftermath.

The perfect excuse to visit a human female and feed.

All his warriors thought so. Grizgunn didn't agree.

He despised the necessity. Hated the forced energy feedings almost as much as being dependent on another. Being with a female never felt good. Too much touching. Too much emotional intimacy. Way too many fucking germs.

A bad taste rolled into his mouth.

Shivering in revulsion, Grizgunn swallowed the burn, then angled his wings and shot into the sky. The shield flickered. Fae magic rippled. Heat raked over his scales as he sliced through the barrier. Ribbons of color followed him up, clinging to the tip of his tail. Ignoring the color burst, he searched for a signal, trying to locate his warriors through the static.

Radio waves squawked.

His sonar hummed. A beep echoed inside his head. The signal whiplashed. Grabbing it by the tail, he looped the stream up and over, folding it like a cable and—

Mind-speak came back online.

"Hakon," he snarled, searching for his friend in the sky.

"Ten seconds behind you."

"Anything?"

"Western range."

Banking into a tight turn, Grizgunn looked to the west. Thunder rumbled above him. Storm clouds pushed the acrid smell of sulfur into his face. The scent of dragon blood reached him as fire lit up the night sky. Long, flaming tails hissing like comets, fireballs criss-crossed, blasting over mountain peaks, dragging brutality across the horizon.

Quiet became a distant memory.

His stomach clenched as screams echoed across the treetops. Fucking hell. Viciousness at its best and worst. So twisted Grizgunn froze in midair, listening to the cries of agony, watching the savagery unfold from five miles away.

Flying in pairs, wreaking havoc and destruction, Scottish warriors snarled while Danes struggled to escape the cruel swipe of enemy claws. Absolute carnage. Utter disaster as he watched his warriors flee in every direction.

No semblance of order. Nothing but panic as the males he commanded lost their minds and forgot their training.

Coordinating their efforts, the Scots gave chase, running his pack into the ground. Or rather, skull-first into sheer cliff faces. The whoresons Cyprus commanded showed no mercy, cutting off escape routes, decimating the younglings he'd recruited, and—

"It's a bloodbath," Hakon said, voice full of shock. *"Griz, we need to—"*

"Don't even think about it."

"Commander—"

"It's done, Hakon. All but over," he said, already backing away.

As he drifted farther from the battle, gaze on the gory sight unfolding across the vale, he reached out with his mind. Six unique energy signals flew onto his mental screen. He exhaled in relief. Thank the Goddess. His personal guard, the warriors he called brothers, were long gone—already outside the twenty-mile marker, flying fast toward Aberdeen.

A wise choice. The city would provide what the countryside couldn't—ample places to hide while his warriors waited for him to arrive. Still...

Leaving his new recruits behind sucked.

He'd worked hard to lure the males to Scotland. Despite their inexperience, he liked them. Had promised each one a home along with an opportunity to train. To grow stronger, be challenged, regain their pride while he decided who made the cut and would be brought fully into the Danish fold.

"*Fuck.*"

"*We might be able save one or two, Griz. If we—*"

"*Leave them,*" he said, leading his friend away from the fight. "*We'll start new...from scratch. Recruit more experienced males.*"

"*The Scots—*"

"*Are brutal. Anyone who flies into that mess isn't coming out alive,*" he said, firming his tone to keep his warrior in line. He understood Hakon's reaction, but dying for a lost cause wouldn't ensure he succeeded in taking back what belonged to him—his ancestral line. Scotland wasn't disputed territory. Cyprus had stolen it from his sire, and was now keeping it from him. No matter how big the setback—how savage the violence— nothing would keep him from reacquiring his birthright. "*Sometimes sacrifice is necessary. Those who matter to us are safe...already headed home.*"

Hakon bared his fangs. "*Shit.*"

"*Go, brother. And don't stop until you reach—*"

A low snarl cut through the air.

An oncoming gust blasted over his scales. Grizgunn's head snapped around. He spotted the Scot fast, recognized the bronze scales and nasty attitude from over five hundred yards away. Rannock, a Metallic with a brutal reputation—well earned, by all accounts. All told to him secondhand, but as he stared the whoreson down, Grizgunn understood none of the tales had been exaggerated.

Velocity on the edge of scale-splitting, the Scot blazed toward him. Shiny scales glimmering as lightning flashed overhead. Talons raised, claws at the ready. Baring his fangs, Rannock exhaled. A glittering mass exploded from Rannock's throat. Bubbling with venom, liquid metal streamed toward him.

Fifty yards ahead of him, Hakon dodged.

Gaze riveted to the blob, Grizgunn counted off the seconds. Three, two, one, and…

Go!

Folding his wings, he dropped like a stone. His spiked tail sliced through the shield. Fae magic sparked like fireworks, painting bubbling liquid bronze every color of the rainbow as it roared toward his head.

Damp air thinned.

Grizgunn ducked.

Liquid metal whizzed over his horns. Droplets splattered across his shoulder, hardening on contact, curling around under the edges of his scales. The acid in the nasty stuff went to work, burrowing through armored dragon skin, sinking its fangs into his muscles.

A wave of intense pain hit him.

His muscles cramped.

The Scot exhaled again. A second bio-toxic stream shot toward Grizgunn.

Fighting through the agony, he flipped up and over. The blob flew past, curled wide, lighting trees on fire as he spun upright.

Blazing a bronze trail across the sky, Rannock rocketed toward him.

With a hiss, Grizgunn tapped into his horns. The tips vibrated. He cranked the valve wide open. A melodic hum hit the air. Musical notes trilled behind him. Poison gas playing in the toxic tune, he turned tail and bugged out behind Hakon, pushing the hallucinogen into Rannock's flight path.

Gas flowed.

Music played.

The Scot twitched.

Looking over his shoulder, Grizgunn watched the whoreson shake his head. Rannock wobbled in midair. His velocity slowed. A second later, he drifted off course and abandoned the hunt, forgetting about him.

Satisfaction rose.

Temptation nudged him, urging him to turn around. Finishing the Scot off wouldn't take much. Affected by the music, the male wouldn't see him coming. Focus locked on his enemy, he debated a moment, then glanced at Hakon. Dark gray scales nearly invisible against the night sky, his friend blasted over the eastern mountain range, exiting the valley, flying hard toward Aberdeen.

Should he...or shouldn't he?

Killing the Scot would be more than just fun. Eliminating one of Cyprus's warriors would send a message, make the commander of the Scottish pack scramble. His eyes narrowed on Cyprus's warrior. Rannock righted his wings. Ash from burning treetops twirling around his bronze scales, he leveled out over the forest. Grizgunn sensed the force of the warrior's will push across the distance. The music ceased as the Scot shook the hallucinogenic spell loose.

Surprise rang through Grizgunn. Holy hell. That was fast. Way too fast.

He should've created a stronger song. Used more powerful gas. Though, as far as failed experiments went, the one that just played out with the Scot was a good one. Knowledge, after all, was power, and now Grizgunn knew the rumors were true.

Metallics commanded powerful magic. Combine that with a brutal nature, strong mind, and...Ja. Maybe getting up close and personal with the bronze-scaled warrior, no matter how incapacitated, was a bad idea without perfecting his bio-toxic composition first.

Dragging his attention from an almost-recovered Rannock, Grizgunn disappeared into the gloom beyond the mountain range. Another night. Another place. Another chance to kill after doing a little more research. In the meantime…

No sense tempting fate.

Or attacking a bronze dragon without a shit-ton of backup.

Next time, he'd do better. Next time, he'd punch up the power. Next time, he'd have the tune-slash-chemical combo he needed—the one guaranteed to drive the Scot over the edge of madness before he flew in and delivered the deathblow.

16

$\mathbf{A}$ngier than she ever remembered being (which was saying something, given her mother gave her ample opportunity to be pissed off every day), Priya sat inside the weird igloo in a chair made of ice, one leg folded under, the other sticking straight out, foot bobbing while she rooted around inside the cardboard box sitting in her lap.

Plastic crinkled as she yanked a biscuit out and took a bite. A very angry one. Half a cookie's worth, at least, stuffing her mouth full. The only way she knew to turn her mind away from the messed-up situation.

Goddamn Levin and his stupid cookies. She hadn't devolved into stress-eating in months.

Finished chewing, she shoved the rest of the biscuit into her mouth. Reaching back into the box, she glared up at the ice dome. Smooth on the inside. Frosted on the outside. A structure designed to keep her in while ensuring she couldn't see out. No cracks in the shell that she could see—or find, and she'd spent the better part of the last hour searching.

Her mouth munched.

Her eyes narrowed.

She wanted to smash her fist through the side of the dome. Hammer it so hard the barrier cracked and ice crumbled. Not that abusing the thing would do her any good. She was halfway up the mountainside, trapped on the ledge where Levin left her. No way of climbing down with her bum hand, or well, any-freaking-thing. Even at her fittest, attempting to free-climb down would end in a very messy death.

Even a world-class climber wouldn't attempt it. Not at night. With a storm brewing. So forget about getting down on her own. Escape was nothing but a pipe dream. A fantasy that included eating the gourmet biscuits left by a jerk who could turn into a dragon.

Priya drew a deep breath.

A dragon who could talk.

Logic rebelled at the idea. Reality interjected, insisting it was true. Her eyes and brain hadn't been lying. Her memory worked just fine. She'd seen him, scales, fangs, wings, and all. Looked Levin in his snow-blue dragon eyes, argued and yelled, while he told her to "be good," then flew away.

"Goddamn him," she muttered, scowling at the picture on the box. The cookies tasted better than they looked. Levin was a huge jerk. How dare he imprison her, then do something thoughtful by leaving her two packages of *these*?

"The motherfucker," she murmured, snatching the water bottle off the floor.

Cold metal settled in her palm.

She stared at it a second, then set the bottle aside and pulled on the straps around her wrist. Velcro hissed. The pressure eased as she slid the cast off her skin. Using her good hand, she pressed her palm to the tips of crooked fingers. Exhaling slow, she straightened each one. Joints and tendons resisted. Twinges of discomfort throbbed through her knuckles. Needing relief, she wrapped her damaged hand around the stainless-steel bottle. She sighed as the chill went to work. Pain downgraded, edging away from hardcore, settling into an annoying ache.

"I'm going to kill him," she said around the mouthful. Flipping the spigot on the cap open, she took swig of water. Chilly fresh, with a hint of lime. Refreshing. All the more reason to dislike Levin.

"I don't care how hot he is, or how much I wanna feel his beard on my skin," she told the box of biscuits. "He's dead when he gets back."

Her threat snaked through the quiet.

Cookie halfway to her mouth, Priya stilled as an awful thought surfaced. Her chest tightened. Swallowing the sudden lump in her throat, she took shallow breaths as disquiet settled deep.

"Dear God," she whispered. "What if he doesn't come back?"

He'd said something about a battle—what she assumed to be a fight with other *dragons*. He could be injured or killed, leaving her trapped and alone. Forever memorialized, buried under ice on the side of a mountain no one ever visited. And honestly, of all the ways she could think of to die, starving to death was her least favorite.

Though being stabbed was horrible too.

Her hand flew to the side of her neck. Tracing the thin scar over her jugular, she shook her head. She didn't want to go there. Reliving the night of her attack never helped. Thinking about it always brought her to the brink, dragging her back into the chaos, making her suffer through the fear all over again.

"No, no, no," she whispered, fighting off panic. "Stay here. Stay *here*, Priya. Don't go back there."

Placing her palm over her breastbone, she pressed in, feeling her heartbeat, using a grounding exercise to help her breathe. She'd been here before. Had spent two years smoothing out the rough patches, using therapeutic techniques, doing mental gymnastics to stave off her nightmares.

Sometimes, though, bad memories got the best of her, dragging her down no matter how hard she fought to keep her head above water.

Taking another breath, Priya struggled to hold the terror at bay.

Think positive. Think positive...think the hell out of positive.

As the words roared through her mind, she popped to her feet. Her boot sole landed on a lemon biscuit. The crunch echoed under the dome. Clutching the water bottle to her chest, she chucked the box of chocolate cookies to the seat, then looked at the lemon-cream ones littering the floor.

Broken bits lay like wounded soldiers on uneven rock.

The messy scramble mirrored her state of mind—cracked but intact. Bruised but not broken. At least, not yet. Much more time spent inside the igloo, though, and the monster lurking inside her would win. Push her so hard, she'd lose it. Go stark raving mad. No amount of gourmet snacks would save her. If Levin ever came back, he'd find her curled up in a ball on the floor, all semblance of the strong woman she'd fought so hard to become long gone.

Closing her eyes, she rested the water bottle against her forehead then rolled it back and forth, using the chill to ground her, breathing through the tightness in her chest, fighting to—

Clang!

Thump!

Bang!

Her eyes snapped open. She glanced up. Rock cracked against the smooth top of the igloo. A dark shadow loomed beyond the wall of ice, huge, hulking, possessing a wingspan that could only mean be one thing.

Relief shivered through her. Anger shoved panic aside.

Gaze narrowing, temper seething, Priya opened her mouth to yell at Levin. A nasty snarl cut her off, stealing the air in her lungs as a huge paw curled over the dome. Talons spread wide, black claws clanked against the surface. Five razor-sharp tips pierced the ice. A guttural laugh sounded as the dragon outside her prison cell moved closer, giving her a better view.

Bright green scales, not pale arctic blue.

Not Levin, but a different dragon, and—

A horned head became clearer through the frosted surface. A flash of fangs. A hiss that turned into another laugh. Her eyes locked on the outline of the dragon, Priya retreated toward the mountainside. Her heart hammered. Her shoulder blades bumped into solid rock as the dragon breathed out.

Mist puffed against the outer shell.

The dome cracked.

Ice began to melt.

Water splashed onto the floor. Rivulets ran toward the toes of her boots. A fissure opened above her. Pressed hard to the back wall, Priya slid sideways, looking for a place to hide. Nothing but a narrow stretch of ledge along sheered-off rock wall. And an ice chair with a low back. No place to run or hide.

Another low snarl.

Her attention shot back up.

Lime-green scales winking through the gap, the dragon tilted his head. A dark eye with a yellow pupil met hers through the crack. An odd shimmer entered his eye.

"Female," the beast growled. "High-energy."

"Drag her out," a second voice said.

Two talons punched through thick ice. Long black

claws curled inward, lethal edges working to widen the hole.

Priya screamed as the ceiling started to crumble. Chunks of ice shattered against the ground. Sharp shards sprayed in all directions. With a growl, the dragon reached through the narrow opening. Avoiding his claws, she threw the water bottle sidearm. Stainless steel spun end over end, flying up through the crack in the dome.

A loud clang reverberated.

The dragon's head jerked to the side.

He turned it back slowly—so slowly her chest compressed, making it hard to breathe as his narrowed gaze landed on her again. He bared a row of sharp front teeth. A hiss left his throat. And she scrambled, rolling under the lethal edge of his claws as he swiped at her, trying to grab hold.

Contrails whistling from his wingtips, Levin rocketed around a sharp jut-out, then flew straight up the cliff. His speed ripped chunks off the mountainside. Rock and ice fell away behind him. The sound didn't register. He was focused, his fear for Priya driving him so hard he didn't hear anything but the voice inside his head calling him a fool.

He should've come back for her sooner.

Hell, he should never have left her at all.

His brothers would've understood. Told him to go, covered his six while he kept Priya close and flew hard for home. The fact he hadn't shamed him.

Priya deserved better from him. He expected more of himself. Nothing mattered more than her safety. The mission would still be there tomorrow. The Danes weren't going anywhere. Months of hunting the bastards made that clear. And yet he hadn't stayed when she needed him most.

The moment he met her, she became his focus, and yet he'd stuck her on a ledge and flown away without explaining...*anything*. He hadn't said a word about energy-fuse, the bond he now shared with her, or the fact he planned to take her home.

What did that say about him?

What kind of male did that to his female?

The question punched through to pierce his heart. His chest tightened. He rocketed around another outcropping. Momentum acted like a slingshot, flinging him up so fast his magic flared. Ice rolled like whitecaps, slamming into the rockface, snarling over the jagged angles in front of him.

Energy-fuse.

Fuck, he was an idiot. So arrogant he hadn't truly understood until now.

The bond between a Dragonkind male and his female was powerful. Undeniable. Unbreakable. A connection that couldn't be downplayed or ignored. He should never have tried. Which made him more than just an idiot. He'd stumbled at the first hurdle. Failed Priya, slid into bad behavior, the second he left her behind, believing he could have it all. Do two things at once—keep her safe *and* join the hunt.

A stupid assumption. One he prayed the Danes didn't make him regret more than he already did.

But as he powered past another vertical rise, Levin knew he was in trouble. Trace energy didn't lie. The warriors ahead of him had deviated from their flight path. A slashing turn sent the pair closer to Priya. He sensed the males slow in flight, then zigzag as they went for her, sensing the powerful bio-energy she threw off without yet being able to see her.

Reaching out with his mind, Levin checked the invisibility spell and—

Fucking hell.

The shell around his female was cracking, the magic no match for the energy Priya emitted like radio waves.

A growl rolled down from up above.

Claws clicked against stone.

Levin heard the ice shell crack. He felt Priya react, sensed her fear as the bond he shared with her flexed. A clang sounded. The sound of feet scrambling. His female screamed. Moving like an inbound missile, he sliced over the last rise.

His mind took a snapshot.

Two rogues perched on the ledge beside the ice dome. One punched his talons through the top. The other sat watching, egging the bastard on as Priya struggled to avoid scissoring claws.

Fury made him fast. Aggression made him brutal as he murmured a command. His ice responded. Magic around the dome flexed. Glacial edges slammed over the opening, trapping the rogue's paw inside. The bastard jerked. Levin didn't stop. He unleashed a wave of magic. The razor-sharp edge sliced through lime-green scales, then cut through bone.

The Dane howled in pain. He yanked his arm sans talons away. Blood arced, splattering over the dome. The arsehole with him cursed, then unfolded his wings, preparing to take flight.

Levin beat him to it.

Without slowing, he hammered him on the flyby. Bright green scales cracked. The male's head whiplashed. Dragon teeth clattered across the cliff, then flew into open air.

Torqueing into a backflip, Levin grabbed one of his horns. The male squawked. Levin unleashed his rage, slamming the Dane's skull into solid rock. Once. Twice. A third time, hearing bone break as the mountainside rumbled.

Snow slid into an avalanche above him.

Unfolding his magic like an umbrella, he protected the dome from harm as he let the dead dragon go and went after the other. Ash blew into his face. With a snarl, he slashed at the blue bastard. Desperate to avoid his claws, the rogue flailed, trying to take flight from other side of the outcropping.

A wall of ice and snow slammed into the Dane.

Reveling in the arctic blast, Levin controlled the

flow, watching the male fall, hearing him hit the bottom of the ravine, burying the bastard alive under hard-packed rock and heavy snow.

"Levin...L-Levin."

The tortured whisper reached him.

Shaking the snow from his horns, Levin landed on the ledge. As he folded his wings, he saw her hand, fingers spread wide, pressed against the inside of the crumbling dome.

"L-Levin."

"Here, Priya."

"Get me out." Her breath hitched. "Get me—"

He murmured.

The spell disengaged. The ice shell surrounding her disappeared as he shifted into human form. Not a wise move under the circumstance—the battle still raged over the valley. His packmates were winning, chasing the remaining Danes north, but...shite. Sticking around wasn't smart. After the fright his female suffered, grabbing her and going would be better, but Levin couldn't do it.

She needed to see his face. Feel his hands on her, register the power of energy-fuse as the bond activated. Absorb the chill in his veins as he wrapped his arms around her. And honestly, after seeing how close the Danes had come to touching her, he longed for the closeness too.

Dark eyes on him, she folded forward as the shield melted.

Conjuring a pair of jeans, he lunged across the ledge. Bare feet planted on cold stone, he reached her before her knees hit the ground. She sagged against him. As he picked her up, she burrowed in, tucking her head under his chin and her face into his throat. Both arms tight around her, he sat down on hard stone.

Cookies crunched under his arse. A lemon scent drifted up.

Ignoring it, he pressed his cheek to the top of her head. "I'm sorry, lass. So bloody sorry."

"I knew it," she whispered. "I knew it."

"What?"

"That it would be soft. That it would feel good."

He blinked. "I'm not following, lass."

"Your beard. I knew it would be soft-scratchy. Not rough."

"Been wondering about that, have you?" he asked, closing his eyes, relief striking so hard he struggled to breathe.

She was all right.

His female was all right.

Shaken, stirred up, still riding the edge of fear, but intact. No rips in her clothing. No marks on her body. No blood on her skin. Uninjured despite her close call with the Danes.

A tremor raked her frame.

Cursing under his breath, he tightened his grip on her.

Curled up in his lap, she shuddered, then drew in a deeper breath. On the exhale, her lips moved against his throat. "I'm really angry at you."

"With good reason," he murmured. "I never should have left you alone. I'm an arsehole for doing it. Forgive me, *zembāla*...forgive me."

Priya didn't answer with words. Bending her knees, she turned toward him instead of away, sliding her arms around his waist. Warm skin brushed his spine a second before she pressed her hands against his bare back.

Her aura sparked with the contact. As the glow brightened, lighting him up from the inside out, his dragon half responded to the buzz of Priya's bio-energy. Raw connection. Pure power. Beauty made real as the mating bond took hold, growing fast, burning bright as the Meridian flared. Electrostatic current flowed through her into him, nourishing his beast, feeding his magic, satisfying a hunger so deep it never went away.

Until now.

Until her.

Pleasure rolling through him in waves, he murmured her name.

"What is that?" Rubbing her nose against his skin, she breathed deep, scenting him, accepting him, the last of her tension fading as she settled like a life-giving angel in his arms. "I felt it before. It's stronger now."

"The bond."

"What bond?"

"The one we now share, Priya. Gorgeous, isnae it?"

"Is it a dragon thing?"

Serious tone. Funny fucking question.

His lips twitched. "Aye, lass—it's a Dragonkind thing. Also, a high-energy female thing when energy-fuse takes hold."

"I have so many questions."

"I imagine you do, but for now..." One hand curled around her ribs, he sent the other in a slow glide up her spine. "Let me look at you."

She shook her head. "I'm good here."

He grinned against her temple. "We cannae stay here, lass."

"Then let's go."

"Need tae look you in the eyes first, *zembāla*," he said, sliding his hand under the heavy curtain of her hair. His palm settled at her nape. Connected at three points—spine, nape, and temple—the Meridian realigned. The stream widened, flowing faster. Her frequency rose to meet his, marrying his life force with hers. Levin groaned in appreciation as his mate shivered in his arms. "Fuck, Priya."

A low sound left her throat as she dragged her nails up his back. Pins of pleasure. Glorious, arousing as hell…if his arse wasn't planted on a ledge in the middle of the Grampian mountain range.

She wiggled in his lap.

"Fucking hell."

"Holy crap."

"Eyes, lass…now," he growled, battling the urge to strip her naked. He couldn't fuck her on the side of a mountain. Not the first time she gave herself to him. Maybe not ever, but…shite. She was killing him. Shredding his control without even trying, so…

Time to move. Before he did something else stupid tonight.

Rolling to his feet, he set her on her own. She swayed. He held her steady, keeping her in the cove of his body as her balance firmed. "Priya—"

Arms still curled around him, breasts pressed to his chest, she tipped her head back. Dark brown eyes collided with his. His breath caught as he ran his gaze over her face. Smudges of black mascara underneath her eyes. Thick lashes all fucked up. Tension gone, body loose, no fear in her minty, wintergreen scent. Zero hesitation as she held his gaze. Cheeks still a wee bit pale, but the energy feeding had helped calm her. Now, after accepting the comfort he offered, she stood strong, aura burning bright, the cables running through her emotional grid anchored and stable.

Another round of relief hit him. The pressure compressing his chest loosened, allowing him to relax.

He tipped his chin. "Good tae go?"

She nodded, then asked, "Where are we going?"

"Home."

Her brows snapped together. "Your home, not mine."

"Aye."

"Figures," she mumbled, taking the hand he held out to her.

Hearing her tone, Levin grinned and, giving her fingers a squeeze, turned toward the cliff edge. "You'll like the lair, *zembāla*. Lots tae do, and my brothers' mates are—"

His sonar pinged.

A harsh buzz lit off between his temples.

The burn ignited instinct. Levin sidestepped, moving Priya behind him. Why? He didn't have a fucking clue. Adjusting his night vision, he stared out into darkness. Craggy mountaintops rising like snarling teeth across the valley. Thick storm clouds brewing. Lightning striking in the distance. No one close. Nothing he could see, but...

His eyes narrowed.

Something buzzed just out range. Not a Dragonkind warrior, an anomaly, one responsible for pushing air into an odd pattern of displacement. Dials clicked inside his head as he fine-tuned his radar. Something blinked onto his mental screen. A second later, the odd signal was gone, but still moving fast, coming toward him and—

"Levin?"

A high-powered whine screamed across the ridge. The air rippled fifty feet from the ledge as a water cannon materialized out of thin air. Five feet wide, seven across, the huge gun took aim, spinning so fast salt water turned into a spear.

With a curse, Levin shifted into dragon form. He heard Priya gasp. Reaching out, he grabbed hold and, cradling her in the palm of his talon, opened his wings. His muscles coiled. His magic roared. Heavy snow swirled as he opened his wings and leapt skyward.

The whirling sound intensified.

Heat rushed over his scales.

Levin banked hard. Too little, too late. Whoever controlled the cannon anticipated his move. The tri-headed spear hit him like a heat-seeking missile. Water split his scales open. The weapon sank deep, punching through muscle, hooking through bone, pushing out the front of his chest.

Pain ripped over his shoulder.

He grimaced, fighting to stay airborne as a metallic scent hit the air. Fucking hell—blood. His *blood*, running down his back, rolling over his chest, splattering over Priya.

Pushing to her knees inside his paw, she screamed his name.

Baring his fangs, Levin twisted, fighting to tear the spear free.

A second spear hit him, piercing his flank. The cable attached to the end loop pulled tight. Leaking blood, power waning, he pulled against the magical-fuel chain. Water hissed. A pulley cranked, dragging him backward through the air. Driving hard with his wings, he tore at prongs, fighting to pull free.

Water began to bubble. Powerful current hissed through the spear, hitting him with electricity. As the jolt sizzled through him, he shook his head. Unbelievable. He'd never seen anything like it. The water taser couldn't be real, but as he got hit with another round of high voltage, disbelief disintegrated beneath a wave of agony.

It was real.

He was in trouble—spiraling inside his own mind as current sapped his strength. His vision dimmed. Seeing nothing but black, feeling nothing but pain, he heard Priya call out. He tried to hang on to her voice. Wanted to stay with his mate forever, but...fuck. She sounded far away. So fucking far away. Beyond his reach as the world went dark and electrified water yanked him out of the air.

18

Following the trail of blood, Callas carried the female down the basement stairs. Thrown over his shoulder, still unconscious from the electrical jolt, she presented no challenge at all. He paid attention anyway, monitoring her vital signs, taking care not to touch her bare skin, making sure he didn't hit her head as he turned on the landing and started down the last set of treads.

Her limbs twitched. Her bio-energy hummed. The low buzz warned him he was running out of time. She'd wake up soon. Start to struggle. Become a problem if she came to before he put her down.

He kept walking, strides even, pace steady, his gaze locked on the injured Scot being dragged down the hall in front of him.

Callas clenched his teeth. *Kólasi*, the scene on the mountainside was a bad one. Not his finest hour. A shitshow he never should've started, never mind seen through to fruition. Finding the Scot alone, without a wing-mate to back him up, seemed like an opportunity at the time. Capturing the warrior, however, was something else entirely. Might be the stupidest move he'd ever made. Then again, it also might turn out to the be the best, given how the Scottish pack operated.

Cyprus ran a tight unit. A close one too.

Information remained thin on the ground, but after weeks spent talking to other Magickind, Callas knew the Scots both fought and lived together. Where? He didn't have a clue. One lair or multiple locations? No one seemed to know, and honestly—he didn't care. Knocking on a Dragonkind commander's front door wasn't part of the plan. To complete his mission, one thing needed to happen. He must sit down with Cyprus and force him to bring every member of his pack along with him.

Nothing more complicated than that. Or, at least, it hadn't been until he let his water spears fly, his electric eels out of their cage, and fried the Scot's circuits to bring him down. Again, a good turn of events...or bad?

Hard to tell. No way of knowing until the Scot woke up and Callas got the information he needed to contact Cyprus.

The brutal commander would come to the table for one of his pack. Would move heaven and earth to find and bring him home. After that, things would get tricky. Cyprus wouldn't take the slight lying down. He'd seek retribution and come after Callas, attempt to rip his head off for hurting one of his warriors.

Something to admire about the Scots.

His mouth curved. He liked the Scottish commander's style. Loyalty and savagery walked hand in hand with smarts and leadership for Cyprus, making him a formidable opponent...and an even better ally. Though, given what he'd done, forging an alliance with the warrior now landed somewhere south of improbable.

Adjusting his hold on the female, Callas watched Rune and Beauregard labor under the Scot's weight. Sandwiched between his friends, arms slung over their shoulders, the male's head hung loose on his neck. The toes of his boots scraped across smooth concrete, dragging through drops of blood, leaving streaks behind him. Not a great sight. The male was bleeding from two nasty punctures, one on his chest, the other through his thigh.

The frost, though, was a good sign.

Frothing above the Scot's skin, arctic mist rolled over stone-block walls, sending comfortable temperatures into a deep freeze as ice dragon magic worked to close his wounds.

"Do something, Beau." His jaw clenched to keep his teeth from chattering, Rune readjusted his hold on their prisoner. "He's a block of fucking ice."

"Stop being a crybaby." Frosty half reveling in the icy froth, Beauregard grinned at him over the Scot's head. "Feels good. No way I'm shutting down the chill."

"This sucks."

"Temperature's perfect."

"Arctic freak," Rune groused, stopping in front of a wide steel door.

"Can't help it if I'm awesome."

Callas huffed. He shouldn't find the byplay funny. Nothing about the situation was laughable, but after years spent trapped in silence, listening to the pair squabble never got old. Every good-natured argument, every playful insult hurled, reminded him he was no longer alone. He wasn't lost and vulnerable at the bottom of the ocean anymore. He'd recovered from the brutality. Found a home with warriors he trusted. Males who supported and accepted him, nightmares, battle scars, and all.

Heavy-duty hinges creaked. The steel door swung inward.

Shuffling sideways, his packmates dragged the Scot over the threshold. Right on their heels, Callas dipped his head beneath the doorframe and entered the lock-down room. The smell of fresh paint and new concrete hit him. His nose twitched as he took in the recent addition to the house on Marlborough Street.

Buried three stories underground, more studio apartment than prison cell, the room contained nothing but a king-sized bed bookended by a head and footboard covered in worn green velvet—a travesty of design he'd picked up on the side of the road. The sheets and duvet cover, though, were brand new—top of the line, soft, thick, glowing bright white beneath a twelve-foot ceiling with recessed lighting.

The door to his left lead to a bathroom. Not fancy, but efficient. Everything a male needed, aside from a window to the outside world and his freedom.

"Toss him on the bed." Callas shifted the female from his shoulder into his arms. Cradling her, he moved around the footboard. Her eyelashes flickered. He nodded in approval. Perfect timing. She was coming around, about to wake up. "On his back."

"Get the first-aid kit, Rune," Beauregard said, rolling the Scot face-up.

Blood smeared across the white duvet cover. Seeing the crimson streaks, Rune pivoted toward the door.

"Don't bother, brother," he murmured, stopping at the side of the mattress.

Rune's gaze snapped toward him. "You speared him good, Cal. He's lost a lot of blood. He needs help."

Preparing to set his passenger down, he glanced at his friend. "He's about to get it."

Beauregard frowned. "What do you—"

"Step away, Beau."

A wave of confusion spiked, coloring the air in the room.

Callas didn't look at his packmates, or take the time to explain. His brothers-in-arms would experience the truth soon enough—see energy-fuse spark and the mating bond take hold the second he placed the female in the Scot's arms.

"Back up." Taking a fortifying breath, Callas held her over the bed. "Get clear."

Boots scuffing across concrete, Beauregard retreated toward the door.

Silence expanded inside the lockdown room.

Leaning forward, Callas brought her closer to the Scot. A stunning glow expanded around her as ice blue filled out her aura. Sparking light pushed into the room. Static electricity hissing against his skin, he set her down fast and backed up quick.

Her brows snapped together.

Her head turned on the coverlet. Half awake, still out of it, she rolled onto her stomach. The Scot growled, becoming restless with her so close. The tattoo on the inside of the male's forearm rippled as he reached for her. Hands rasping over duvet, she moved, crawling toward her mate and—

His fingers curled around her wrist.

A starburst flashed into the room, strobing across the walls.

Rolling into her, the Scot wrapped himself around her, pulling her deep into his body. He tugged at her clothing. She buried her face in his hair, grasping, clinging, tangling her legs with his. Hands found bare skin. The Scot set his mouth against her pulse point. Drinking deep, he fed fast, drawing the healing energy he needed through her as the Meridian flared, and the pair sank into the cosmic stream.

Holding on tight, she raised her chin to give her mate greater access, aura pulsing so bright Callas looked away, protecting his light-sensitive eyes.

Witnessing the connection, Rune blinked. "What the fuck is that?"

"Energy-fuse," Beauregard said, awe in his tone.

"Impossible, Beau. The bond between mates is a myth."

"Look at them, *mon ami...*" Beauregard paused to flick his hand toward the bed. "Then tell me energy-fuse doesn't exist."

Dragging his focus from the bed, Rune frowned at him. "How did you know?"

Callas shook his head. He didn't want to talk about Amelia. He lived with her loss every day. Yearned for her return, and the gift of energy-fuse, when he woke in the evening and struggled to fall asleep during the day.

Memories of her tormented him. Relentless. Brutal. The grief came no matter how hard he fought to keep it at bay. Rehashing the loss wouldn't help. Talking about her would only make the pain burn deeper.

The Scot moaned against his female's throat.

"Out. Now." Chest so tight it hurt to breathe, Callas turned on his heel and headed for the door. He couldn't watch them a second longer—or trespass more than he already had. An energy feeding between a Dragonkind warrior and his mate was sacrosanct. A private affair to be respected, not witnessed. "We'll come back later… talk to him once she's given him what he needs to heal."

Beauregard pursed his lips. "Do we really want him at full strength?"

"I vote no." Grabbing the handle, Rune swung the door closed behind him. The quadruple deadbolts on the door fell like tumblers, clicking through the quiet. "A Scottish warrior at half strength will be easier to break."

Nasty tactics, but a strategy worth considering.

Turning the plan over in his mind, Callas weighed the pros and cons, then murmured his wishes. The electronic keypad next to the door lit up. He punched in the code with his mind. The electrical grid hummed to life, surrounding the lockdown room on all sides with high voltage.

A necessary precaution.

Electricity weakened a Dragonkind male's magic. No matter how powerful outside the prison cell, the Scot wouldn't be able to use his sonar. No way for him to connect with his pack through mind-speak. No way for him to break out of the electrified cage. A comfortable one with top-of-the-line mattress and Egyptian cotton sheets, but still...

The experience wouldn't be a pleasant one.

Having one's freedom stolen never was, but after weeks of getting nowhere with the Scottish pack, Callas was desperate enough to give a bad idea a good try. Which meant the warrior would remain in lockdown until he received the information he needed to move on—one way or the other.

And if he didn't?

A number of different scenarios spun into his head.

Jogging up the stairs, Callas cracked his knuckles, praying he never came close to using the most brutal option on his list. He didn't want to do it. Under normal circumstances, he'd refuse to use an innocent female as leverage, but his future hung in the balance. Locating the son he'd sired with Amelia meant everything, so no matter how abhorrent the idea, he'd use what he had to get what he needed...

The Scottish warrior's mate included.

19

Finished checking the bathroom for an escape route, Priya switched off the light and came back into the room. Her gaze went straight to the man lying on his side in the middle of the bed. Blood was smeared on the duvet beneath him, but none on his body. Expression peaceful, but sleeping hard. Chest rising and falling in a steady rhythm. Nothing but smooth skin poured over heavy muscle, all trace of his injuries gone.

She swayed as relief gripped her.

Reaching out, she grabbed the side of the door jamb. Levin was all right. His color was good. He looked relaxed, none the worse for wear after enduring horrible physical trauma.

Thank God...thank God...thank God.

As the chant echoed through her mind, she shook her head, trying to clear it. Trying to figure out why she felt so strongly about him. Trying not to lose her mind as a weird hum came through the walls, sounding like thousands of angry bees.

Her gaze cut to the steel door ten feet from the foot of the bed.

The hum intensified there. Every time she got near it, her skin prickled. Which made touching it a bad idea. Not that she could open the stupid thing anyway. The dark metal panel covered in medieval-looking rivets didn't have a doorknob.

Panic chased shivers down her spine.

Inhaling deep, Priya exhaled slow. In. Out. She needed to keep breathing, stay calm, continue to work the problem and search for a way out or...

Her focus cut back to the bed.

She could wake up Levin.

Chewing on her bottom lip, she stared at him. God, he was beautiful. Strange to think of him that way with so much blatant masculinity on display, but...he was— without a doubt—totally, unbelievably *beautiful.*

The urge to touch him tolled through her.

Her feet took her to the side of the bed before her brain told her to go. Standing there watching him sleep, she wondered about him. About so many things —all the hows and whys of his ability to be two things at once. Both man and dragon. Both breathtaking and brutal. Both hardcore and kind.

Setting her knee on the mattress, she leaned forward onto her good hand. The closer she got to him, the more the blood in her veins sang. Something about him called to her. And when he touched her, her world tilted, righting on its axis, making the jagged pieces inside her settle back into place.

She closed her eyes

God. It had been so long. So motherfucking long since she'd felt like herself. Strong. Bold. Smart. Striking in her own way, no matter what others thought or ridiculous beauty standards said. She might have scars on her skin now, but she wasn't any less of a woman.

Any less beautiful.

Any less worthy.

Any less capable of moving through the world on her own terms.

Somewhere along the way, she'd forgotten that valuable lesson. She'd spent too much time listening to other people, allowing their prejudices to color the way she saw herself. The epiphany seemed to come from nowhere. But Priya recognized its origin. The way Levin looked at her—held her, spoke to her, protected her—shook the realization loose, dragging the truth up from deep inside her.

Sliding deeper into the bed, she murmured, "Levin."

The whisper sounded loud in the buzzing silence.

He didn't move. Didn't twitch, so—

She nudged him. Cascading prickles swept over the back of her hand. A rumble came from deep inside his chest as his hand flexed. Shifting on the sheets, he reached for her, exposing the inside of his forearm. She paused, fingers hovering above his arm, arrested by the sight of the tattoo inked into his skin. Black and gray gradient. Details both stark and stunning. Each line drawn with care and precision. Beautiful to look at, and...

Her lips parted as she focused on the woman's features. Nestled inside a skull with twisted horns and hollow eye sockets, the image took her breath away. Not just any face—*her face*. The resemblance was unmistakable—same eye shape, cheekbones, mouth and... Priya swallowed past the burn rising in her chest...the scars. The marks on her skin were drawn in ink too. The thin one on the side of her throat half-hidden by thick braids. The slice bisecting the edge of her left eyebrow. The healed, nearly imperceptible, nick beneath her lower lip.

Her likeness inked into Levin's skin, in Viking-inspired artwork that was both beautiful and fierce. A woman of strength, power and drive. A warrior princess drawn in her image, which caused all kinds of questions to file into her head. First—did he truly see her that way? Second, how in the hell had he known what she looked like?

She understood energy-fuse. It was hard to deny. She felt her connection to him with every breathe she took, but...*this*. His commitment to her, inking her into his arm before ever meeting her. God. The idea he'd wanted her that much —needed her that much—astonished her. Pleased her. Encouraged her to be bold and explore as awe whispered through her.

Swallowing past the knot wedged behind her breastbone, she trailed her fingertips over the ink. As she traced his tattoo, marveling at the details, Levin made another low sound. Delight curled through her as the rumble became continuous. Her mouth curved. Hmm, how adorable. He was purring like a big cat. *Purring* every time she touched him.

Charmed, she shuffled forward on her knees. Her hand trailed up his arm, over his shoulder, then jumped to the long strands of his hair. She twirled blond tendrils around her fingers, brushing it off his forehead, before switching tact. Caressing his jaw, she stroked down his throat, enjoying the soft-scratchy texture of his beard against her skin.

"Levin," she said, a little louder.

The enthralling purr turned into a growl.

"We're trapped in here. I can't find a way out. You need to wake up."

His brow furrowed. He shifted on the sheets.

Priya stroked him again, becoming bolder, moving lower, exploring further, and—

Big hands grabbed her.

The world went topsy-turvy. White walls whirled into a blur as Levin rolled her up and over him, tumbling with her across the bed. She landed with a soft thump, back to the mattress, hands clenched in his hair with him on top of her. Hooking a hand behind her knee, he spread her thighs and settled his hips in be-tween. Another purr sawed out of him. His beard rasped against her chin. He pressed in, grazing her throat with the edge of his teeth.

Heat settled low in her belly.

Her voice came out raspy when she breathed, "Levin."

His head came up. Shimmering, snowy eyes caught hers a second before he nipped her lip. She gasped. He invaded her mouth, kissing her deep and wet, so in-tense, so crazy-beautiful, she didn't resist. Didn't want to. Priya egged him on instead. She needed more of his taste, more of his touch and weight and scent, every-thing all at once as he drove her into desire so fast she became restless beneath him. Demanding. Needy. Lost to sensation and the intensity of what he made her feel.

Holding on tight, she rolled her hips into his, asking for more.

Levin didn't disappoint her.

He gave her everything she wanted, then fueled the fire. Tugging on the front of her jeans, he popped the button open. A sharp tug on her zipper, and his hand went down and in, sliding through the wet gathering between her thighs.

Another purr rumbled from his throat.

A mew left hers as he caressed her, touch firm, rhythm just right, pushing intense pleasure toward ec-stasy with each mind-blowing stroke.

"Yes," she moaned into his mouth. "Goddamn, motherfucking, *yes*."

He kept at her.

She responded in kind, panting, writhing, whim-pering as he buried two fingers deep. His thumb flicked over her clit. Bliss picked her up. Rapture stampeded through her, driving her over the edge so hard, she shattered into tiny pieces. Nothing but stardust, she lost track of him, relaxing so completely she floated into nothingness.

His touch grounded her, keeping her safe as she came down. Slowly. A little at a time, feeling Levin all around her. His scent. His weight. His hands—the fingers of one fisted in her hair while the others remained deep inside her. Priya hummed in appreciation. God, that felt good. It was nice, the kind of claiming gesture made even nicer as his mouth traced her cheekbone. A soft sweep across her eyelid. A gentle kiss to the bridge of her nose. So soft. So sweet.

A long shudder rolled through her.

Levin lifted his head.

She opened her eyes.

Intense snowy-blue ones met hers. "That's what you get when you wake me up."

"Then I'm waking you up every day."

His eyes flashed in appreciation. A smile spread across his gorgeous face.

Stunned by the sight, she concentrated on catching her breath. "Though a brilliant and welcome surprise, that wasn't what I was angling for when I touched you."

His fingers flexed inside her. "You sure?"

"Yes," she gasped, tilting her hips into his caress. "I mean, I love orgasms as much as the next girl, but..."

Showing no mercy, he stroked over a sensitive spot inside her.

She bit back a moan. "Levin—"

"You feel good, lass. I need tae give you another," he murmured, his gaze roaming her face. "Didnae see the first one. Felt it. Tasted it on yer tongue, but didnae get tae *see* you come apart."

"But—"

"Hold on."

"Levin, you need to focus."

"I am, lass."

"Not on… God," she said as he shifted onto his forearm, making hard muscles ripple. Distracted, unable to stop herself, she slid her hand out of his hair, down the side of his neck, and over to his shoulder. Wow, he was strong. Beautiful to look at, arousing as hell as his gaze tracked down to where his hand lay buried inside her jeans. His fingers moved again, making her breath catch. "I don't know if you've…um, noticed. I tried to tell you earlier, but we're trapped in—"

"I know where we are, Priya."

"The thing is—"

"Sun's coming up. It'll be hours before the bastards come back."

"Who?"

"I'll explain after you come for me again."

"Levin—"

"And I've finished fucking you."

"Seriously—"

"I need tae get my fill, *zembāla*. Three or four times should do it."

Priya blinked. *Three or four times?* "Are you crazy? We've been taken prisoner!"

"Is that going tae change in the next few hours?"

"I don't know."

"It isnae," he said, thick brogue rolling, making her quiver. "The hum in the room is electricity. I cannae magic my way through it, lass. We're stuck here until I negotiate our way out, so we're gonna fuck hard, then talk a while. I'm gonna learn about you. You're gonna learn about me. Then we'll fuck again. And probably some more after that. Deal?"

"You're sure you can't get us out of here?"

"Not right now."

She pursed her lips, wondering if she was crazy for wanting do what he said, in the precise order he said it. "That's…ah, a lot of fucking."

"Look at you, lass. You're gorgeous. Lots of fucking is in order."

The compliment slid deep, applying salve to old wounds, wiping every insult away, banishing the darkness to open her up to the light. Tears stung the corners of her eyes. She didn't want to cry, or for him to see how much his words meant to her, but…

No such luck.

He saw her clearly. Read her expression as his own softened. With a murmur, he dipped his head. His mouth brushed hers. Once. Twice. On the third pass, he flicked her lip, scraping over the scar, then delivered his taste with the tantalizing sweep of his tongue.

She clenched around his fingers.

He grinned and asked softly…ever so softly, "Deal, Priya?"

Holding his gaze, she hesitated, making him wait. Why? No good reason. She wanted him. Longed for the closeness. Needed the pleasure. Lying naked, tangled up with him in bed while talking, sounded fantastic. After years of being ignored and sexually deprived, the intimacy of it appealed to her. Then again, everything about Levin did.

From the moment he rescued her from the warnocks, she'd sensed the shift. Felt the pull. A deepening of her intuition. The heightened spark of awareness. None of it could be denied, her fierce attraction to him least of all, and as he waited for her answer, an intense craving rumbled through her, shaking her foundation.

She wanted to take a chance and trust him. With more than just her body. With all of her. Without fear of rejection getting in the way.

The powerful need wasn't normal.

With him kissing her, Priya didn't care.

"Okay," she whispered. "Deal."

He purred her name.

She shivered in delight. God, she loved it when he made that sound. Loved it so much she basked in his touch, gloried in his kisses, giving up control as he dragged her into rapture, and she reveled in the descent.

20

Enthralled by the look on his mate's face, Levin moved inside her. Dark eyes heated. Lips parted. Panting against his mouth as he cupped the back of her knee and pushed her thighs wider. The shift in position changed the angle. She moaned. He ground in, rubbing over a sensitive spot, feeling her quiver, watching arousal heighten the color along her cheekbones. One hand buried in his hair, the other angled across his lat, she rolled her hips into his thrusts, meeting his gaze with a challenge in her own, playing a game he refused to let her win.

Though it was fun watching her try.

Priya wanted it to last, was committed to driving him wild, curious to see what would happen if he lost control. Kissing him deep, she hummed against his tongue, making him want to give in. Her spirit enlivened him. Her passion humbled him. Her stamina stunned him, pushing him hard, forcing him to admit her plan was working.

The sight of her, the scent of her, the sounds she made while he fucked her, drove him to the edge, threatening to push him over, pull him under, and—

She rippled around him, clamping down *tight*.

Pleasure ripped up his spine. Levin groaned and…

Fucking hell.

The Goddess of All Things must love him.

His mate was glorious. An incredible lay. So hot for him, he struggled to hold back. To give her the pleasure she deserved before he took his own. Mind-blowing. Incredible. Priya tipped the scales, the pleasure so intense it approached the boiling point. *Again.* Which was fucking crazy, given he'd already loved her three times.

The first two rounds, he'd taken her hard and fast—in ways he'd discovered she liked. The third time, he'd lain back and let her ride, undone by the way she moved, dark hair tumbling around her as she took him back to paradise.

Bliss. Pure heaven.

Right now, though, he rode her gentle instead of wild. Or, at least, was *trying* to—reveling in her sleek heat, listening to her moan, indulging in a slow, lazy loving. Something he needed after the intensity that had gone before. Even though she was pushing him, Levin knew his mate needed it too. Lots of eye contact. Loads of time spent in exploration with drugging kisses and languid touches.

Each sweeping caress carried the same message—acceptance and love, the deep-seated devotion he felt for her laid bare for her to see.

He sensed her disbelief at his intense attraction to her. Read the surprise in her eyes as he made her his, and he became hers.

Priya didn't believe she was desirable. Complete bullshite. A lie she'd been taught through experience. The scars on her skin had no doubt caused males to turn away. Idiots like that never bothered to look for hidden treasure. Too busy looking for perfection, they missed the point, lacking the depth necessary to see a female like Priya for what she was—a gift so precious, she was utterly unique. Smart. Strong. Spirited. *Desir-*

able. A woman built to be challenged in life…and bedded as often as possible.

He liked everything about her. The more often he took her to bed, the faster she would believe his need for her was real. It would take time to convince her, but he relished a challenge, so instead of telling her with words, he showed her with his body—touching her with reverent hands, kissing her deep, loving her sweet, addicted to the way she looked at him.

Planting his forearm in the bed, he put more power into his next thrust. A low whimper escaped her. He growled in return, watching, memorizing, thrilling to the feel of her. He powered in again (and again), keeping the rhythm slow, but each thrust heavy. Deep stroke followed by slow, beautiful grind. Levin smiled as her need deepened, and she clutched at him.

"Levin."

"Stop holding back."

"But—" Breath rasping in her throat, she tipped her head back. Her chin came up as she undulated beneath him. "I don't want it to end."

"This is only the beginning, Priya. You'll have me again," he said, brushing his mouth over hers, stroking deeper, harder, faster. "Often. I promise."

She made another low sound.

"Let go."

"God."

"Let go, *zembãla*. Give it tae me."

"Not yet. Not yet. More…just a little bit more."

Done indulging her, Levin gave her to the count of ten, then dipped his head. His teeth grazed the tip of her breast. He bit down, held her captive between sharp edges, heightening her pleasure with the threat of pain.

She moaned.

Showing no mercy, he tongued over the furled bud, then suckled her hard.

Her whole body tightened, bowing into a beautiful

arch. A brutal shudder raked her. "Motherfucking fuck…fuck, fuck, *fuck!*"

Overwhelmed by her, needing relief, he upped the pace, hammering into her, taking what she wanted him to have.

Bliss.

Torture.

Absolute heaven.

The burn flickered through him. She clenched down on him again. He rode her harder, faster, through her second orgasm, then reached for his own. Plunging deep, he stayed planted and pressed his face in her throat. Hoarse sounds left him as he throbbed inside her.

Priya went limp beneath him.

The room settled into silence.

Sated, more relaxed than he ever remembered being, he settled in, giving her his weight. Minutes ticked into more before she started playing with his hair. Legs curled around his thighs, she twirled her fingers in the ends, then shifted underneath him to rub her cheek against his jaw.

Fingertips dancing, she ruffled his beard. "I like this."

His mouth curled. "You made that clear when I had my mouth between your legs earlier."

"You gonna let me return the favor?"

"You enjoy giving head?"

"I like the taste of you. I like the sounds you make. I like the way you use your body. Odds are, 'cause of all that, handsome, I'm going to enjoy sucking you off."

Muscles low in his abdomen tightened in anticipation. "Then I'm gonna let you return the favor."

A soft laugh escaped her. "When?"

"Later."

"How much later?" she asked, wiggling underneath him.

"A wee bit later…after I get some answers."

She tensed, taking his words as a warning. Smart lass, given the topic next up on the agenda.

Sliding his hands between her and the bed, he rolled. He settled on his side, head to the pillow, and, pulling her close, hooked her knee over his hip, then reached for her damaged hand.

"Don't."

"Trust me." Moving slow, touching her gently, he captured her wrist, pressed his palm to hers, then slid his fingers over her crooked ones. She flinched and tried to pull away. He held steady, refusing to let her go…or allow her to avoid the conversation. "We've talked a lot today. About my tattoo and what having you inked into my skin means tae me. About yer job, yer podcast, yer life in London. All the op-eds and articles you've written over the years."

"Yeah," she said, tugging on her hand. "Lots of different things."

"I know you donnae want tae, but Priya…" He laced their fingers together, feeling the uneven lines of once-broken bones under her skin. "We need tae talk about this."

"Levin—"

"I need tae know what happened, lass."

"Long time ago."

"How long?"

"Long enough."

"Priya," he said, a warning in his tone.

She closed her eyes and turned her head away.

Cupping her cheek, he brought her back. "Eyes, *zembāla*."

She exhaled a shaky breath, then gave him what he asked. Dark eyes met his, the suffering in them so stark his heart clenched. A terrible ache tightened his chest as compassion swelled, making him want to take her pain away.

He murmured her name.

"Two years," she whispered. "Feels like forever ago, and yet it's not. I think about it every day. I go to bed with it. I wake up with it. It's always there."

Intuition sparked.

He tapped into her bio-energy, feeling her anxiety spike, getting a sense from the chaotic thoughts tumbling through her mind. "You were chasing a story—"

"A big one."

"And got caught in the crossfire."

"I put myself there, Levin."

"How?"

"Rumors had been flying for months. The police weren't looking into it, so I tapped some of my sources, learned a few things. Started figuring out the rest." Her brow furrowed, she shook her head. "It was bad, Levin. But then, that shit always is."

He raised a brow.

"Sex-trafficking ring. Underage girls. Big operation pulling girls from lots of different countries."

"Fucking hell."

"I know," she whispered. "I was in over my head, and knew it, so I got in touch with a detective inspector at the Metropolitan Police. Everything I dug up, I started feeding to him. He pulled a task force together. With both of us on the street, we started to figure out how the operation worked—when and where the parties would take place. He busted up a couple of parties, rescued some girls. Once he started interviewing them, the pieces started falling into place."

"But you dinnae leave him tae it. You kept digging."

"*Teenage girls*, Levin. I couldn't let it go." Her hand flexed in his. "I thought I was doing it safe Being smart. Protecting my sources, insulating myself by giving everything I got to the police, but..." She swallowed. "I got distracted, so I wasn't careful enough."

"How did that happen?"

"Papa died." Making a pained sound, she blinked as tears filled her eyes. "Massive heart attack. He was there one minute, gone the next."

"You were close," he murmured, feeling her pain.

"He was my biggest fan," she said, trying to smile, failing miserably. "Always told me I could be anything I wanted. Could be *anyone* I wanted. He gave me permission to be who I am, and you know, since my mother's the opposite, I needed that growing up. He believed in me, and that helped me believe in myself. So when I lost him..."

"You went reeling."

"The grief swallowed me whole. Then my mother started in, wanting me to get married. My father was the buffer, the person who kept her in check. With him gone, she became relentless, every day, always after me." Wiping tears away, she shrugged. "And Levin, I'm not proud of it, but to get her off my back, I accepted Franklin's proposal, knowing it wasn't right, but between my mother's constant harping and trying to help those girls, I caved under the pressure."

"Understandable, Priya."

On a roll, she kept talking. "And instead of doing my job, I'm distracted as hell, pushing sources too hard, not being careful enough. Next thing I know, I'm being dragged out of bed in the middle of the night and treated to the business end of a ball-peen hammer."

The news shook rage loose, making him snarl, "Names."

"Levin—"

"I need names, Priya."

"Listen—"

"Where are they now? In prison?"

"No."

He bared his teeth. "What the fuck?"

"I saw their faces. CCTV caught them leaving my place, but the footage was grainy, not a hundred percent clear. And the evidence was—" She made quotation marks with her fingers. "—*lost* en route from the crime scene. Due to lack of evidence, the CPS declined to prosecute."

"Payoffs?"

"Probably, but I can't prove it."

Fury turned into the need for revenge. "Names, Priya. I'm going tae find the bastards and—"

"I got lucky, handsome." Holding his gaze, she touched the scar on her throat. Over her jugular. One he knew had been made by a knife. "I live next to a pair of nosy neighbors. They heard noises and called 999. The EMTs got to me fast."

"Saved your life."

"Yeah, but not my career. I haven't worked a big story since. Too scared. I didn't leave my flat for nearly six months after it happened," she said. "So I started my true crime podcast. I like it. I'm good at it, but I miss helping people. So, when I started getting calls from some guy named Shell, and all the information he gives me turns out to be accurate, I keep taking his calls. He helps me solve some cold cases. I ask him about everything, including a cult up near Aberdeen. He tries to warn me off, but I've got the scent, and I *know* he has more to share. People are being hurt, so I convince him to meet me, and...here I am, locked in a room with you. And you know what?"

Seeing her lying on her bedroom floor in his mind —battered, broken, close to bleeding out—Levin couldn't answer. He needed to find and kill the bastards. Wanted to smash their bones. Watch their blood flow. Bury them six feet under.

Unable to find his voice, he gathered the dark strands of her hair in his hand. Playing with the soft tendrils, he shook his head in response to her question, hoping it would be enough to keep her talking.

"I like that you want to avenge me, Levin, but it's

over. I'm tired of thinking about it. I want to move on, not go back there."

"Good, 'cause you willnae be going back...*ever*."

"I don't want you to go either."

"Too bad."

Worry shifted out of her eyes. The hum of her bio-energy slid back in as amusement lit her expression. "Are you always this stubborn?"

"I just learned arsehole males took a hammer to my mate's hand and tried to slit her throat." She flinched on "slit." Brushing his thumb over her cheek, he soothed her with his touch, but kept going, determined to drive his point home. "The ones responsible are going tae bleed. *Bleed*, Priya...rivers of fucking blood."

"I don't get a choice in it?"

"Not in this."

She pursed her lips.

He kissed the irritated look off her face. She reacted like she always did when he put his mouth on her—she turned into heat lightning, cracking through his defenses with the sweep of her tongue. Addicted to her taste, he rolled onto his back, pulled her astride him, and took the kiss deeper. With a wiggle, she lifted up and slid her hand between their bodies. Her fingers danced across his abdomen, working their way down, and—

Heavy footfalls sounded in the hallway.

Fingers tangled in her hair, he sat up fast, his gaze on the door. He waited a beat. Another soft thump. A scraping noise, then the zing of a cord being unwound and something being plugged in. Holding Priya astride him, he tilted his head and listened harder. The rasp of boots across concrete came next. Two, maybe three, males gathering in the hallway outside the cell.

Priya shifted in his lap. "What is it?"

Gripping her hips, he rolled out of bed, taking her with him. "Get dressed, lass."

"Are they coming?"

"They're already here."

"Shit."

"Calm, *zembāla*." Positioning himself between her and the door, Levin conjured his clothes. Jeans and a long-sleeved Henley settled on his skin. Steel-toed boots on his feet, he listened to her grab her clothes off the floor. Fabric rustled behind him. As she got dressed, he glanced in her direction. "We talked about this, remember?"

"I remember." Pulling an elastic from her pocket, she raked her hair away from her face. A quick twist, and she tied the thick mass into a messy bun. Moving behind him, she wrapped her arms around his waist, pressing her front into his back. "Just give me clear signals, okay?"

Drawing a measured breath, he nodded, thanking his lucky stars. His mate—so incredibly smart. Tapped into his frequency, she read him well, knowing what he needed before he asked her to give it.

"Keep yer eyes on me, Priya. Move when I tell you tae move. Run, if I tell you tae run. No hesitation, aye?"

"Got it."

He murmured his approval.

The hum of electricity cut off.

Deadbolts turned, clicking through the quiet.

Rolling his shoulders, Levin cracked his knuckles, then flexed his fingers—ready for anything, praying he spoke true when he assured Priya he could negotiate his way out of the mess as hinges creaked and the reinforced steel door swung open.

21

As Callas dipped his head under the lintel and stepped into the lockdown room, eyes the color of snow with a hint of sky greeted him head-on. No give in the male's expression. Much different from the last time he saw him. Then again, maybe that wasn't fair.

The Scot had been bleeding and unconscious at the time, not as he was now—stance set, body strong, muscles loose, ready for anything as he waited for Callas to move deeper into the room. So much patience. An admirable amount of control. The male stood firm in the face of bad odds, giving nothing away.

Brave. With a hint of crazy, and…

Absolutely fucking dangerous.

A split second, that was all it took, for Callas to know the Scot was lethal. A warrior of immense strength and skill. The powerful magic he threw off like radiation after nuclear fallout cemented what he already suspected—like Callas's own son, the Scot had been born of a high-energy female.

Interesting information, given one stood at the male's back.

Not that he could see much of her.

Keeping her behind him, the Scot shielded her with

his body. She let him, staying close to his back, giving her male what he needed to keep her safe. Or as safe as possible under the circumstances.

Boot soles thumping across concrete, Callas moved farther into the room. Rune and Beauregard filed in behind him as he stopped at the foot of the bed. Messy sheets tangled up on the mattress. Crumpled coverlet thrown onto the floor. The scent of sex in the air. His mouth curved. Good. Very fucking *good*. The female had not only healed her mate, but spent the last few hours fucking him—accepting him, satiating him, dispelling the sexual need that always made males testy.

Relaxed from bed play, the Scot would be much more willing to talk.

Pivoting to face the pair, Callas leaned his hip against the footboard. Worn forest-green velvet rasped against the faded denim of his favorite jeans. He settled in, crossing his arms over his chest, keeping the vibe casual, like he was kicking back to chat with an old friend.

Snowy eyes narrowed on him.

"Callas," he said, gaze locked on his guest/prisoner. Could go either way. Guest if the male agreed to his proposal. Prisoner if he didn't. "Formerly of the Grecian pack."

"Levin," the Scot said, speculation firing in his eyes. "Greece. Ye're a long way from home."

"Necessity brought me here."

Levin's brow quirked. A gesture that asked for more information without using any words.

Kólasi, two minutes in the room, and he already liked the male. Something about Levin rang true, making Callas realize he'd met a warrior with as strong a will as his own, one he could respect in the same ways he did Rune and Beauregard.

Silence stretched as he stared at Levin, and Levin stared back, waiting him out.

Callas's lips twitched. "Heard that about your pack."

"What's that?"

"You're all hardcore."

Levin shrugged. "If you're going tae do something, best tae do it right."

Losing the battle with amusement, Callas grinned, then got down to business. "Been trying to contact your commander a while."

"Hell," Levin muttered. "Ye're the one clogging up my inbox."

Callas scowled. "You haven't answered."

"No time. Shite's been intense."

"Grizgunn," he said, giving it his best guess.

"Among other things."

"*Kólasi*," he growled, struggling to keep his cool. Clenching his teeth, Callas flung his hand out, gesturing to the lockdown room. "All of this could've been avoided. A few keystrokes. It would've taken you no time at all to answer, and I wouldn't have been forced to—"

"Fuck off, Callas. I donnae answer tae you."

Fair enough.

No need for him to go nine rounds with Levin about that fact. Dragonkind packs who controlled territory were a law unto themselves. The Scots owed him nothing. Not their time or attention. Cyprus wasn't obligated to cooperate with others of his kind. And yet Callas's temper spiked anyway, threatening to boil over. All his messages ignored. So much time wasted. He wanted his son. He longed to meet him. Needed to make it right for Amelia, in honor of her memory.

Dead or not, his female would expect that from him.

The urge to do violence bubbled up. Battling the need to rip Levin's head off, Callas bit down on a snarl and—

"Cal," Rune said. "Steady."

Moving away from the door, Beauregard got close, prepared to lock him down if he lost control.

Watching the interaction, Levin tilted his head. "Why do you want tae meet my commander?"

Taking a deep breath, Callas regained control. "I'm looking for someone. A Dragonkind warrior."

"And you think Cyprus knows where he is?"

Callas hesitated, wondering how much to share. He'd decided how best to proceed before arriving in Scotland. His strategy had been set from day one. Relaying the bare minimum—holding information back—always worked best. But as he held Levin's gaze, instinct surfaced like a buoy inside him, leading him in different direction.

It was time.

Time to be honest. Time to put all his cards on the table. Time to find a way to trust someone other than his brothers-in-arms.

Silfer had fucked him, setting him free while tying his hands.

He'd been searching for so long without success. Something needed to give. Intuition insisted the Scottish pack held the key. Maybe with Levin's help, he could bypass Silfer entirely. Do the fucking over for a change. Get what he needed without ruining a warrior's life by feeding him to the Dragon God and—

"Tell him, *mon ami*," Beauregard murmured, Gallic accent thicker than usual. "The Scots are connected in ways other packs aren't. You know it. It's the reason you brought him here."

Turning his head, Callas frowned at his friend.

"Something tae know about me, Callas," Levin said, tone soft, inviting trust. "I'm my pack's intelligence officer. All information runs through me. I relay it tae Cyprus, so—"

"Fuck," he breathed. "You're the one I need to ask."

Levin nodded. "Who're you looking for?"

"My son."

"Water dragon?"

"Yes."

"How old?"

"He'd be thirty-five now."

"Why do you want tae find him?"

Confused by the question, Callas frowned.

Seeing his reaction, Levin wiped the confusion away fast. "Do you wish him harm?"

He growled, insulted, disheartened by the assumption.

Though he understood why Levin made it. Rumors about water dragons ran rampant in Dragonkind circles. Most of what was said about his kind wasn't good. Lies written into ancient lore. None of it true, as far as he knew, but given water dragons were rare, the fallacy males of his subset killed their offspring, refusing to allow any of the children to be born, continued to feed the urban legend.

"Callas," Levin murmured, dragging him back to the present.

"He's my son."

"Do you plan tae kill him?"

"Fuck no," he said through clenched teeth. "I want to meet him. Get to know him. Claim him as my own. My mate, Amelia, would've wanted that...would've expected me to shield and protect him. I didn't get the chance, failed him as a sire before he was even born, but I'm free now. I want the chance to make it right...to make it up to him."

"She died?" the female asked, the compassion in her voice edged by sadness. Shifting sideways, she peaked out from behind Levin. Eyes dark as night landed on Callas. "You lost her?"

Agony tightened his chest. Numbness spread the

way it always did when he thought of his female. Callas cleared his throat. Unable to stay still, he uncrossed his arms, flexed his fingers, trying to work feeling back into his hands as he pushed away from the bedframe.

Silence spiraled through the room.

Callas let it lie, refusing to answer, his focus steady on Levin.

The male's gaze raked his frame. "Do you wear a watermark?"

The astuteness of the question made Callas pause. The Scot knew something—must have met or seen a water dragon to know about the tribal markings. Unique to his subset of Dragonkind, the tattoo arrived with a warrior's *first shift* into dragon form, magic etching a pattern into his skin. One that was passed from sire to son.

"Show him," Rune said.

Callas hesitated a moment, then reached over his head. He dragged the t-shirt off and tossed it onto the bed, exposing the swirling black ink that stretched across his torso, over his chest, curling over his shoulder, down his arm to his elbow.

Studying the tattoo, Levin took a long look, then met his gaze again. "Your wren—"

"Is gone." Another brutal loss, one Callas mourned every day. Ephie had been beautiful, a female miniature dragon of unparalleled viciousness...and absolute loyalty. His friend and companion, a constant presence in his life until the sea-witch took her way. "She starved to death during my imprisonment."

"Oh, no."

"Priya," Levin murmured in warning.

"Well, it's sad," she said. "I mean, I don't know what a wren is...and even though I want to tie ropes to Callas's arms and legs, attach them to four horses, and watch them rip him apart for injuring you and tasering me—"

Beauregard snorted in amusement.

Rune grinned.

"A small zap," Callas said in protest. "Just enough to knock you out."

Her eyes narrowed on him. "I felt it. You didn't. It wasn't a *small* zap."

"Apologies," he muttered, fighting the sudden urge to laugh. A miracle, given his tension and the topic.

"Fine," she snapped, telling him it wasn't *fine* at all. With a scowl, she turned her attention back to her mate. "But Levin…his wren died too. He lost them both along with the chance to raise his son. It's sad."

The Scot sighed. "Fucking hell."

"And besides…" Pausing for dramatic effect, Priya stared at him, then returned her attention to Levin. "I'm not getting evil vibes from these guys. I don't like their methods, but you wanted a diplomatic solution to this mess. You have one now."

Looking harassed, Levin glared at her over his shoulder.

Widening her eyes, she held her ground, refusing to look away.

Callas interrupted the standoff. "You know something."

Snow-blue eyes sliced back to him.

"You know where he is," he said, reading the shift in Levin's eyes. "You've seen him."

The Scot's jaw flexed, making his beard twitch. "I cannae guarantee anything. I need tae speak with my commander. Make sure. Clear a few things."

Heart thumping, hope rising, Callas reached into his back pocket. Pulling a cordless phone from his jeans, he tossed it in Levin's direction. "Make whatever calls you want. Door'll stay open. Meet us upstairs when you're done."

The Scot tipped his chin.

With a quick pivot, Callas turned and strode out of

the room, leaving Levin to make his calls, praying his trust wasn't misplaced, and he hadn't just made a huge mistake.

Sitting at the kitchen island, Priya flipped the laptop open. Carefully. The computer was beat to hell. The backlit screen was scuffed and scratched, the keyboard wonky, the H, Z, and 7 keys missing, little stubs sticking up, making it difficult to type.

Afraid to add insult to injury, she stared at it, uninjured hand hovering over the keys, wondering what happened to the poor thing. Had Callas been using it while engaged in hand-to-hand combat? Or maybe he'd punted it from room to room in the rundown Victorian he shared with his friends.

Both assumptions seemed logical, given he'd tossed the Mac onto the orange, throwback-to-the-seventies countertop, and grunted for her to "have at it" before exiting the room.

Not a big computer guy.

"Obviously," she muttered, shifting on the rickety stool.

As metal brackets squeaked, she took a chance and tapped on the cracked trackpad, using a single fingertip and light pressure.

She held her breath before, wonder of wonders, the laptop fired up, allowing her to move the arrow over an icon sitting at the bottom of the screen. She tapped again. The internet browser opened, prompting her to input an address.

Picking her way across worn keys one-handed, she signed into her email account. Nothing but busywork while Levin finished his phone call. She heard the low rumble of his voice coming from the other room. He hadn't wasted any time getting her out of the lockdown room into the house above stairs. Or making her a ham and cheese sandwich in the travesty Callas called a kitchen before leaving her to do her thing at the island.

He'd taken off to do his.

Almost an hour later, he was still at it. Talking to Cyprus. Connecting with his packmates. Tapping a bunch of his other contacts, asking about a guy named Henry Biscayne. She didn't know who that was, but listening to Levin fire up his network gave her a little thrill, making her realize he collected sources too—cultivated relationships, dug up important information, keeping his finger on the pulse, just like her. Though his intelligence-gathering operation was much more extensive than the one she'd built in London.

Her mouth curved as she listened to his muffled voice roll into the kitchen, then returned her attention to the screen. With a flick, she scrolled down, reading through messages sent from people who listened to her podcast, *Salt in the Wound*. Some just talked about how much they enjoyed the cases she highlighted every week. Others wrote in to tell her about the odd, scary, and often hilarious events that happened to them (or a relative, both living and dead) in the hopes she'd include it in one of her hometown episodes.

Ghost stories. "Saved by my dog" stories. Escaped convict stories. Natural disaster stories. "Caught having sex during a bank robbery" stories. The occasional cold case inquiry. You named it, she got it. Always bizarre. Always fascinating. Always the highlight of her week.

Some crazy, seriously weird stuff went on out there in the world.

The thud of footfalls sounded. Beat-up wooden floors creaked.

The swish of the swinging door rushed across the kitchen.

Twisting on the wobbly stool, praying it didn't give out and dump her on the floor, Priya glanced over her shoulder. She shivered, getting another thrill when Levin's eyes landed on her. He moved out of the doorway, past acres of scarred cabinetry, around the end of the island.

She expected him to stop next to her.

He scooped her off the stool instead.

Big hands cupping her ass, he pulled her in tight, breasts to chest and core to groin with him. The scent of him all around her, she wrapped her legs around his hips, loving the way he felt in her arms. His beard whispered over her cheek. His teeth grazed her bottom lip. Need rose hard. She made a low noise as he turned, set her on the countertop, and, hand buried in her hair, invaded her mouth.

She hummed in approval.

He deepened the kiss, acting as though he was starving, as though the hour he'd spent away from her had been too much. As though he couldn't get enough.

It went on a while.

Long enough for things to go from heated to scorching.

She got her hands under his t-shirt. He slid one of his down the back of her jeans. And as he drank deep, taking her to the brink, wonder curled through her. How had she lived without this? How had she not known the right man would feel this way? How would she ever be able to go back? To return to the life she knew knowing Levin was out in the world somewhere, living his life, while she went on alone without him?

Priya didn't want to think about what happened next. She wanted to pretend, to hold on to the impossible, forget that she came from one world, and he existed in another. But as he retreated, breaking the kiss, she mourned the loss of him, now and in the future.

Resting his forehead against hers, he opened his eyes. "Hey."

"Any news?" she asked, running her fingers over his beard.

Levin shook his head. "Biscayne's in the wind."

"No sign of him at all?"

"Nay," he muttered, sounding annoyed, coming in for another kiss. A gentle one. Being affectionate, getting close and staying close. Something she liked a lot about him. "Didn't check out of The White Hare, but all his luggage is gone. Ferguson, Kruger's mate, is picking over the Parkland, but so far, nothing. The bastard orchestrated the showdown in the cemetery, but I doubt he'll show tonight."

"Why would he do that?"

"No clue. Doesn't bode well, though. He might be lying about what he knows, but I cannae take the chance. I need tae take the meet, be there just in case I'm wrong and he shows up at the inn," he said. "So, I cannae wait for nightfall. I need tae get home, lass. Rannock's already in the Hog."

She blinked. "The Hog?"

"A helicopter. Relic from the Cold War," he said, mouth brushing hers. "Ran likes ripping shite apart and putting it back together. He restored it. Now, it's pure luxury topped by rotor blades."

"Are Callas and the boys going too?"

"Aye. Plenty of room in the Hog," he murmured. "Cyprus wants tae meet him. See what's what, make a decision about whether tae help or not from there."

"Which way are you leaning?"

"Too soon tae tell."

"But you're keeping an open mind?"

"I'm standing in the male's house, arenae I?"

"Good," she said, hoping things went Callas's way.

"Not really." Nudging her chin up with his nose, Levin raked his teeth along her jaw line, then moved down. She shifted against him, restless and wanting as whiskers rasped over her pulse point. With a hum, he kissed the scar on her throat, then raised his head. "I hate flying in the fucking Hog. My wings are better."

"Daytime really sucks for you, doesn't it?"

"You've no idea. If sunlight wasn't poisonous tae my kind, I could watch you bathe in it topless."

She laughed.

A mischievous glint in his eyes, he watched her, then slipped his hand under her shirt. With a quick tug on her bra, he bared her to his touch then cupped her in his calloused palm, making her breath hitch as he added the roll of his hips, rubbing the seam of her jeans against her clit, teasing her with the promise of him.

"Levin—"

"No time tae fuck you now, *zembāla*. Later, though," he growled, backing off, allowing her to regain her composure. "Gonna watch you ride me again, then flip you over, set you on yer knees, and take you from behind...hard."

"Oh my God," she muttered, part shocked, mostly turned on.

He grinned, kissed her again, then gestured to the laptop. "What're you working on?"

The quick change of subject stymied her for a second.

He waited.

She pulled it together and answered, "Listener emails. Fans of the podcast."

"How many you got?"

"I hit twenty-two and half million downloads last month."

"Jesus, lass."

She smiled at him. "It's grown fast. Has become more than I can handle on my own, so last month, I hired Aspen. She's helping me with production—editing and sound engineering, doing some other bits and bobs too. But I like reading the emails, so that's all me. There are always really good stories in there."

"You should write a book."

Surprise flickered through her. Her mouth fell open. "Write a book?"

"Aye," he murmured like it wasn't the craziest idea in the world. "Pick a true crime case that fascinates you. Do the research. Investigate it, interview people, fill in whatever information might be missing. You donnae need tae be there in person, lass. Interviews can be done via videoconference."

Not knowing what to say, she stared at him.

"You're a writer, Priya."

"I'm an investigative reporter, Levin."

"Same difference."

"Not really."

"How many articles have you written?"

She shrugged. "A lot."

"Then you're a writer," he said, giving her a squeeze. "Not much of a leap from op-eds in newspapers and magazines to writing nonfiction, true crime books. It'll take you longer, for sure, be more of an involved process, but I'll set you up inside the lair. Make sure you've got yer own space. A proper studio for yer podcast and—"

"A proper studio?"

"Aye. Won't take long, lass."

Won't take long.

It certainly hadn't.

In less than a day, she'd fallen so hard—wanted to stay with him so badly—the intensity of it scared her. It wasn't normal. Nothing about the situation made sense. Neither did how she felt about him.

From the instant she met him, fierce attraction had taken hold, dragging her into a place she didn't understand but, somehow, knew was meant to be.

Everything about him felt right.

She belonged with him. In his arms. In his life as partner, lover, and friend. But more shocking than that was the fact he seemed to feel the same way about her. He wanted her with him so much he'd been thinking ahead—preparing, planning, providing what she needed to be happy in his world.

Joy bubbled up inside her. Her throat tightened. "I'm not going back to London, am I?"

He frowned. "Do you want tae?"

"No, but Levin…" Her voice cracked as emotion scored through her. Clenching her good hand in the front of his t-shirt, she held on, hope becoming a living, breathing thing inside her chest. "You and me—it's happening really fast. Like, at the speed of light *fast*."

"That scares you?"

"Yeah."

"Good. Means ye're not stupid, Priya." Gathering her hair in his fist, he bunched it into a bun at the nape of her neck. His other hand settled against the small of her back, holding her secure, keeping her close, communicating his certainty through touch. "We're new, really fucking new, and in the human world, that means no guarantees. But what you gotta get is, ye're in my world now. Rules in yer world donnae apply tae mine. The bond we share is solid. So deep, so profound, so fucking strong, my feelings for you are undeniable. One day, one month, a year from now or a hundred of them, that won't ever change. And I know it comes as a shock, but Priya, ye're mine, and I'm yours. We belong together. You cannae deny you feel the truth of it down deep in yer bones."

"I can't deny it," she whispered. "I won't even try. It's just…overwhelming."

"You'll get used to it."

Maybe, but probably not. She had a feeling Levin would keep her on her toes. Her mouth curved. Something for her to look forward to…along with the man in her arms.

"So, Aberdeen?"

"Aye, lass."

"Looks like I'm going on another adventure."

Amusement sparked in his eyes. "And writing a book."

"Maybe."

"For sure," he said, before kissing her soft and sweet. "My mate—so fucking smart, so very talented, pure beauty in my arms, my dream lass come tae life. You can do anything you put yer mind tae, Priya."

Tears pooled in her eyes.

Blinking them away, she pressed her face into his throat and burrowed in, needing every inch of her up against every inch of him.

"No limits, *zembāla*." Setting his mouth against the top of her head, he wrapped both of his arms around her, holding her tight. "Start believing it, lass, 'cause with you, I already know that it's true."

God. He was killing her. Her trajectory didn't matter anymore. Levin was right. She could do whatever she put her mind to—no limits. No more bowing to expectations. No more boundaries hemming her in. No more fear keeping her out.

No limits.

Not anymore.

When it came to him and her, she was free. Free to be herself. Free to be with him. Free to let go of the past, do as Levin asked, and *believe*.

23

LONDON, ENGLAND - TWO WEEKS LATER

He found the bastards sitting at the back of a gentlemen's club. Decked out in designer suits, ties loosened, fat arses planted in plush club chairs. Surrounded by five other males, drinking scotch after enjoying a couple of lap dances. Unaware they were both about to die.

Martin Lanigan. And his cockroach of a sidekick, Barney Applecross.

The names of the males Priya refused to speak out loud. The ones Levin had found all over the case files and scribbled in the lead detective's notebook. Not information he should have, but Ivy (Tydrin's mate) was brilliant with computers. In less than an hour, she'd hacked into Metropolitan Police servers and pulled everything he need to hunt down his prey.

Names. Addresses. Personal information. Mug shots. Interrogation tapes on Priya's case. No stone left unturned. Now, he knew everything about Lanigan and Applecross, though not why they'd turned into arseholes who stood for nothing, preferring to lead lives of crime.

A mystery for their mamas to solve.

Levin didn't care. He hadn't flown all the way to London to dissect the pair's psyches.

He scanned the large alcove the males sat in again—a soaring archway with massive doors fronting the space, both thrown wide open, allowing the group a good view of the main stage where two pretty females danced.

Clean, classy, a high-end club with deep pockets. An establishment owned by the syndicate Lanigan worked and killed for.

His eyes narrowed on the pair.

Arrogant pricks. Both prime suspects in his Priya's attack…and guilty as fucking sin.

No one he talked to had disputed the facts.

The detective inspector who'd caught her case made no bones about it, speaking plainly on the phone. The CCTV footage backed up the copper's certainty, showing the pair leaving her building the night of the attack.

Lanigan and Applecross were the ones. The ones he wanted. The ones who needed to pay. The ones he had in his crosshairs from his position at the bar.

Aggression thrummed through him. A chill shimmered across his skin, making his palms itch. He could throw his ice daggers from where he stood, but…

What fun would that be?

Hands on was always more effective. A lot more fun, too. To avenge his mate, he needed to get up close and personal. He wanted both Lanigan and Applecross to know the reason he was there. Planned to watch as the bastards bled out, doing to them what they'd done to Priya.

With very different results.

Neither male would make it to a hospital in time.

Standing between two stools, Levin picked up the squat tumbler and downed the rest of his drink. Ice-cold vodka burned down his throat. The second the empty glass settled back on the bar top, he heard, "Need another?"

With a flick of his fingers, he sent the tumbler spinning across polished wood, then pushed out of his lean. His attention landed on the bartender, a pretty redhead dressed to kill in a low-rise tank top. Moving in a way he knew upped her tips, she stopped in front of him, bottle of Vusa already in hand.

She pointed to his glass.

He shook his head. "Not tonight."

"I'm off in five minutes," she said, hazel eyes fixed on him. "Up for a private party?"

"I've got a lass of my own, *talmina*," he murmured, then pointed to Tempel. Shoulder blades flat against dark paneling, arms crossed over his chest, his packmate stood in the shadows, in a spot guaranteed to go unnoticed by patrons, watching Levin's six, even though he didn't need backup. "My friend, on the other hand..."

He let his comment hang like smoke in the air.

A dimple creased her brow as she looked in the direction he pointed. She scanned the space beyond the bar. It took her a half a minute to find his packmate, but...

Her eyes widened when she found him. "Nice. He's free?"

"As a bird."

"Enjoy the rest of your night." Flashing him a smile, she wandered down the bar, her gaze glued to the big American holding up the wall. "I have a feeling I'm going to."

The corner of Levin's mouth tipped up.

Heavy muscle shifted on the stool next to him. Forearms planted on the rounded edge of the antique bar, Kruger turned his head. Eyes dark as the devil and twice as mean met his. "You done fucking around?"

"I'm savoring the moment."

"And my mate likes tae fuck first thing in the morning. No way I'm missing that," Kruger growled. "Get on with it, brother."

With a tip of his chin, Levin turned away from the bar. Halfway across the club, stride even, pace unhurried, he started the countdown.

One second…

He skirted the main seating area.

Two seconds…

He walked past the end of the T-shaped stage.

Three, four, five, six, seven…

He paused under the arch, on the lip of the private room. Seven pairs of human eyeballs turned in his direction. He let them look. Anticipation rose. Aggression swelled. He allowed the moment to stretch, then stepped over the threshold and murmured a command.

Magic swirled out to do his bidding.

Double doors swung closed behind him.

The lock clicked.

Males cursed. Chair legs scraped across the wooden floor. Time slowed. Levin moved, walking forward as the first male engaged. He didn't use his magic. He deployed rage, ducking, spinning, striking without mercy, cutting a swath through the room.

The temperature dropped. The smell of blood burned through the frosty air. Grunts sounded. Hisses of pain followed.

Bodies hit the floor.

Applecross attacked from behind. The lethal edge of a blade glinted.

With a quick pivot, Levin spun beneath the strike. On the upswing, he grabbed the bastard's raised arm and squeezed. The blade toppled, falling end over end toward the floor. With a snarl, he snapped Applecross's wrist, changed his grip, and, exerting brutal pressure, shattered every bone in the bastard's hand.

Applecross opened his mouth to scream.

Levin gave him no chance.

Conjuring twin ice daggers, he sliced up and across. The sharp cry died on a gurgle. As Applecross collided with the floor, Levin turned toward his last target. To the one most responsible. To the male he knew enjoyed slitting people's throats. He didn't delay. Each stride measured, he crossed the room as Lanigan fumbled to pull a pistol out of the back of his pants.

Levin flicked his wrist. His ice dagger whistled through the air.

Lanigan jerked, gun clattering to the floor, hand flying to his throat. Blood running between his fingers, the bastard hit his knees and toppled sideways. The thud of his boots muffled by the music beyond the doors, Levin stopped next to him. He stared a moment, watching Lanigan's lifeblood flow, then sat down with his back to the wall beside him.

He met the male's shocked gaze.

He watched his mouth move. No sound came out, but Levin understood.

"Priya Burman."

Recognition sparked in Lanigan's eyes.

"I am the reckoning," he whispered. "You never should've touched her. Now, I've made sure you'll never touch another living soul."

The light faded from Lanigan's eyes. His head lolled to the side.

Taking a deep breath, Levin pushed to his feet and crossed to the door. His brothers-in-arms were waiting outside. His mate was waiting for him at home. He'd righted the wrong done to her. Time to put the past behind him and help Priya build the future she deserved.

24

FIVE STORIES UNDERGROUND — THE
DRAGON'S HORN PUB, OLD TOWN,
ABERDEEN

The faint smell of fresh paint in the air, Priya stood inside her new office. The place she would conduct videoconference calls. A space she would do research in, write the scripts for her podcast in, along with whatever else struck her fancy. A room she was tempted to set on fire just to watch it burn if Levin didn't return home soon.

He was late. Really, *really* late.

And despite the fact none of the guys wanted her to, Priya knew exactly where he'd gone. Against her express wishes, Levin had flown to London.

Now, she was angry with him. Again. Really, *really* angry with him.

She'd told him no. She'd asked him to leave well-enough alone. Even without proof in hand, she knew he hadn't listened. Which made her want to punch him and kiss him at the same time.

Irritation flickered through her.

She scowled at the glossy surface of her new desk, then pursed her lips.

Maybe she'd do both. Punch him first, then kiss him better after she inflicted the damage.

Crouching in front of a box, she flipped the top open, and grabbing the antique lamp by the throat, freed it from its confines. Antique glass sparkled under recessed lighting, sending an array of color across white oak paneling.

She touched the shade with her fingertip. The hinges tilted. The angle of the light changed. The rainbow brightened, reminding her of the one she'd seen in the Fairy Glen. Taking a deep breath, Priya closed her eyes. Two weeks since the warnocks attacked her inside the Rover. Two weeks of going to bed and waking up with Levin every day. Two weeks that qualified as the best of her life.

Pushing to her feet, she pivoted toward her desk. A second before she slammed the lamp down on the corner of it, she stopped. The lamp was a gift from Levin. A beautiful piece unearthed by Lapier (a Numbai, full of unflagging energy, made of pure awesomeness, also the Scottish pack's go-to-guy). She scowled at the thing. It was perfection, a fantastic addition to her new office-slash-state-of-the-art-sound studio.

Her annoyance faded a little.

With a sigh, Priya set the lamp down with care. She adjusted it, finding the perfect spot, then shook her head.

Levin hadn't lied. He'd done what he promised, giving her an incredible space. Elegant, modern and comfortable. Contemporary aesthetic combined with old world charm, a theme that continued throughout the underground lair. She loved her new home. Loved her new family. Felt more comfortable living among Dragonkind warriors than she ever had growing up at home.

Still...

The fact Levin had left the lair without telling her what he planned bothered her.

Setting her hand on her hips, she stared at the pale green paint above the wainscoting. Calming color, something she needed while she arranged furniture and practiced her speech. The one she planned to deliver when Levin got home. The one in which she told him he'd crossed a line, hiding his intentions from her, doing something that dragged the past back into her present.

"Goddamn it," she muttered. "I'm over it. I need for it to be over."

With him in her life, she was healing. Going long stretches, entire days, without thinking about the attack. His ice dragon half helped. The chill in Levin's touch lessened the pain. Without the constant throb to remind her, she'd settled into her new life without missing a beat—or a single regret for leaving the old one behind.

So, yes. Absolutely.

It was done. She was *over it*. Now, she needed him to be over it too.

Priya frowned. How did she help him get over it?

A good question. One she'd asked her new girl posse.

Mated to the other Scottish dragon warriors, the girls had accepted her without hesitation, offering friendship, welcoming her into the fold, helping her adjust to life inside the lair— becoming something of a sounding board.

Elise, Amantha and Ivy advised her to let Levin be Levin, and leave it alone. Cate and Nicole disagreed, encouraging her to proceed with caution, but not to let it go. The crux of their argument—Levin needed to learn to take her wishes into account before he flew off half-cocked. And Fergie?

Plugging the lamp in, Priya shook her head.

New innkeeper to The White Hare, Fergie was a badass. She wanted Priya to hold Levin's feet to the fire and nail his ass. A lovely thought, but then, she suspected given Fergie's occupation—the fact she kept a variety of vicious Magickind in line for a living—her new friend simply enjoyed a good showdown.

She pursed her lips.

A showdown might end up being fun. A showdown might be exactly what Levin needed to—

The phone on her desk rang.

An old school landline, given cellphones didn't work inside the lair. Too deep underground. Too much magical interference for wireless signals to get through.

Priya hesitated. She should probably let it go to voicemail given her current mood, but with all the changes, she and Aspen needed to connect, hammer out the details, and get the podcast back on track and into production.

On the fourth ring, she snatched the receiver from its cradle. "Hey Aspen, just give me a—"

"Priya, my darling."

She blinked. "Mum, how did you get this number?"

"It's the same one I always call—your mobile."

Goddamn Lapier. The Numbai was too efficient by half.

She'd been working with him on logistics. He'd taken care of everything—arranging the extra line, and as evidence was suggesting, ensuring all calls to her cellphone got forwarded to the new landline.

"Listen, Mum—"

"Have you looked at the bio-data I sent you?"

"What's bio-data?" she asked, already knowing she was going to regret it.

"Honestly, Priya. You must pay more attention." Her mother sighed in exasperation. "How do you expect your life to improve if you don't stay on top of things?"

"Mum," she said, a thread of warning in her voice.

"I sent you the bio-data the matchmaker pulled together yesterday. She found three good matches for you. Pick one of the three, darling. I will begin planning the wedding."

"I told you I don't need a matchmaker."

"You do, Priya. With your *shortcomings*, how else will you make a suitable match?"

Taking a deep breath, she waited a beat, then said. "I have a man, Mum."

A pause. A lengthy one, followed by…

"What?"

"It's serious. We'll get married when the time is right."

"A British man?"

"Scottish, actually."

"Priya," he mother said, tone sharp with disapproval. "A man from Scotland isn't good enough for—"

Tingles swept over the nape of her neck.

A delicious shiver rolled down her spine.

Her mother kept talking.

Tuning her out, Priya glanced over her shoulder, and…hmm. There he was—big body taking up all the real estate on her threshold, gorgeous snowy eyes riveted to her.

"Goodbye, Mum." Hanging up, she set the handset on the desktop, not back in its cradle, ensuring her mother couldn't call back. The conversation was done, all contact with Saanvi Burman now over. Or at least, it would be once she told Lapier to change her cellphone number.

Shoulder propped against the jamb, Levin crossed his arms over his chest and tipped his chin. "That didnae sound like it went well."

"It never does. Unlike Papa, Mum's never been my biggest fan."

"I hate that for you, lass."

"Can't change it, never could."

"I still hate it," he said, a muscle twitching in his jaw.

Her nose started to sting, heralding the threat of tears. "Levin…"

Picking up the warning in her tone, he pushed away from his lean against the door frame.

"What have you done?"

"You know what I've done." Gaze moving over her face, he studied her. "On a scale of one-tae-ten, how pissed are you at me right now?"

"Thirty-two-and-a-half."

His lips twitched.

Her eyes narrowed "Not funny, handsome."

"You're adorable, lass."

"Are you trying to make me throw my fabulous new lamp at your head?"

"*Zembāla*," he said, expression moving from amused to serious.

Seeing the shift in his mood, she held his gaze, and her ground, killing the urge to cross the room. To go to him. To reassure him. To slide into the shelter of his arms and soothe herself.

"I'm past it," she said, trying to make him understand. "I was on my way there before I met you. I wouldn't have left London to meet Shell, if fear still had a hold of me. But now, with you, it's completely gone. The terror along with the nightmares are gone, so now, I need the rest of it to be over too."

"It had tae be done, Priya," he murmured. "After what they did tae you, I couldn't live with the knowledge the bastards were still breathing, walking around on this earth, free tae enjoy their lives and ruin other people's."

That last bit got to her.

He'd been avenging her, absolutely. But she also knew that what he'd done tonight was bigger than her. It was about honor. It was about protecting others. It was about ensuring bad men paid for their bad acts. It was about Levin being Levin, doing what he needed to be able to live with the fact she'd been hurt before he met her, and there wasn't a thing he could do about it.

Her chest tightened. "Handsome—"

"It's done, *zembāla*. Over. I can let it go now."

"Please," she said softly, reaching her damaged hand toward him. "Come here."

With a quickness that defied reason, he came unstuck and moved toward her.

One moment, he stood at the door, the next she was in his arms. Pressed tight. Held secure. Protected, loved and cherished. She stayed that way with him, face pressed into his throat, seconds turning into minutes, relief rolling through her as he set his mouth to the crown of her head.

"Ye're the best thing that's ever happened tae me, Priya."

She leaned back a little, putting pressure on his arms. His grip on her eased. Raising her hand, she met his gaze and cupped his jaw. Fingertips dancing across the scratchy softness of his beard, Priya let the last of her anger go. He was who he was. She needed to let him be just that—a man of integrity who protected his own.

Her thumb drifted over his bottom lip. "I love you."

"Fuck, Priya."

"I love you so much sometimes it's hard to contain."

"Jesus, lass. I love you too."

"I know," she whispered. "You show me every day. I don't like that you went after them, but I absolutely understand it. But more than that, I appreciate it. You're right. I wasn't the first one they hurt, and I wasn't the last. But now, they'll never hurt anyone again. Honor demanded it. You saw to it. And I love you for it."

He made a low sound.

Sliding her hand into his hair, Priya drew his head

down hers. She kissed him soft. She kissed him sweet. And like he always did when she touched her mouth to his, Levin kissed her back.

EPILOGUE

THE PARKLAND - ON THE GROUNDS OF THE WHITE HARE

Standing on a distant hilltop with binoculars in hand, Henry Biscayne looked down on the rambling hotel. Huge fucking place. A throwback to another time, the Victorian mansion with its wide windows, granite façade, and disjointed peaked roofline, sat on a gorgeous piece of property surrounded by manicured gardens and dense forest. Not that he cared about the building, its history, or the complex of stables nestled in the woods behind it. His gaze stayed on the large outdoor terrace. On the wide expanse of flagstone lit by fancy-ass garden lights where tables were being set up.

An army of waitstaff came and went, marching in and out a series of French doors thrown wide, hands full of the necessary accoutrements. White tablecloths on round tables that sat eight. Fine china place settings fit for a king. Flash silverware. Crystal goblets winking under the glow of lamplight and a blood moon. The low-lying floral arrangements, though, put the cherry on top—pink and white roses in full bloom with sprigs of delicate greenery.

The setup must've cost a fucking fortune.

"Swanky affair. The cocky bastards." Colored by an

odd accent Henry couldn't place, the voice came from behind him.

Scanning the area around the raised terraced, Henry didn't bother to turn around. "Weddings usually are, Tamarack."

"In your world, maybe," the Druid muttered. "Not in mine. We just get it done."

"Without asking for consent, I would imagine."

"You imagine right." A low chuckle, then, "Keeping to tradition, strong ancestral bloodlines, matter more than individual preference."

"I'm aware." Or at least, he was now.

His transformation from human into Vampiric Fae Prince (an aberration most Magickind considered an abomination) changed his view of things. A great many of them, actually. Studying the ancient lore had helped. Coming to terms with his pedigree along with the magic he commanded had taken time, but he understood now what most Magickind ignored—direct descendance and strong family ties mattered. Pure bloodlines birthed empires, ensuring power stayed in the hands of those best equipped to wield it.

A novel idea, given he'd been raised in the United States where democracy was revered, the voices of the many more important than the few. Not that politicians—or the general public in his country of origin—acted like it anymore. It was a shitshow. A free-for-all, individualism over the collective good, profit over people now.

Henry didn't mind. He'd always been a take what he wanted, fuck everyone else in the process kind of guy. His daughters understood his leanings—had always accepted him for who he was, helping him in the grift, doing their best to shield him during the long cons he excelled at orchestrating.

His mouth curved up as he thought of his butterflies.

Such good girls. He missed them so much, which made what he planned even more necessary. He wanted Nicole and Cate back, sure, but more, he *needed* them. Everything hinged on family—on his ability to manipulate the present and ensure the future. Consolidating his power through his daughters was the surest way forward, the only way for him to secure his claim to the vacant Fae throne.

Monarchs, after all, required heirs.

The Fae blood that now flowed through his veins put him at the head of the line. He might not have been born of kings, but the infusion of ancient magic made him one, changing a common thief into royalty, allowing a new dream to be born.

Frogmore (his valet) wanted him to forget about Nicole and Cate. More opinionated than he should be for an indentured servant, the guy never shut-up, telling him to leave the girls alone. He kept harping about allowing them to be happy, informing Henry no one who understood the Magickind world tangled with Dragonkind. Especially dragon warriors who wielded immense power in ways the Scottish pack did.

Problem was…

Henry didn't give a shit. Those were his girls. *His.* And he *needed* them now more than ever, given he could no longer sire children. Irritation rippled through him. In the world he now inhabited, his new-found infertility posed a serious problem. In order to ensure the continuation of a dynastic line, a ruler must produce a male heir. A task he could no longer perform. Not that he hadn't been trying.

Since digging himself out of the dirt in Savannah, he'd slept with countless women. So many he'd lost track, often taking more than one to his bed at a time. Months had passed without results. No pregnancies. Not even a single scare or close call. But worse, no one he consulted could tell him why.

All his parts worked. His sperm count remained high, and yet no babies.

He scowled into the binoculars. Goddamn witch. The spell she'd cast, along with his involuntary sojourn inside her coven, had changed him in ways he still didn't understand. An itch of unease crawled across the back of his neck. Maybe, his inability to get a woman pregnant stemmed from the rewiring of his DNA. Maybe he simply needed to wait for his body to adjust to the magical infusion. And maybe, that excuse amounted to a load of horse shit.

The Blind Witch hadn't been kind.

As was her way, she'd been brutal, forcing the change, giving Henry something he hadn't known he wanted. Now that he owned it, though, he refused to let power go. Or allow the opportunity to slip through his fingers. His girls possessed what he needed to get what he wanted—his DNA and fertile wombs. Once the blood rites were performed (breaking the mating bond with their dragon warriors), the transformation would take hold, turning Nicole and Cate from human to Fae, providing him with the building blocks to start a new monarchic line.

Footfalls whispered through the long grass.

Tamarack stopped beside him.

Lowering the binoculars, Henry glanced at him. "Has your informant been in touch?"

The Druid nodded. "Ascot sent word yesterday."

"Good." Henry rolled his shoulders to break the tension. Taut muscles protested. Ignoring the discomfort, he pointed in the direction of The White Hare. "Who's getting married?"

"Double feature," Tamarack said. "The innkeeper and her dragon warrior. Levin and his mate."

"When?"

"Night after tomorrow."

"The Danes are in play?"

"Set to meet me on the edge of the Parkland. Just before the ceremony is scheduled to begin." Reaching down, Tamarack tugged on a piece of long grass. The blade came away in his hand. He folded it up and over, in between in fingers, braiding it into a complicated knot. "Coordinated attack. With your vampire horde, Legion and the Danes aligned, the Scottish pack won't stand a chance."

"Grizgunn knows not to touch my butterflies?"

"Your daughters won't be harmed," Tamarack said. "Both will be delivered to you as promised."

"Be sure about that, Druid." Henry flicked his fingers. Heat flared at the tips. The binoculars disappeared into thin air. Tucking the pair back into his mental vault, Henry turned away from the wedding preparations and strode down the other side of the hill. "One scratch, a single bruise on either of them, and I'll make you pay."

Tamarack's throat bobbed.

Henry read the extreme nervousness. With a silent hum, he drank in Tamarack's fear, feasting on it, allowing it to fuel him.

Showing respect, Tamarack stayed two steps behind him. "My laird?"

"What?"

"I've done all you've asked," Tamarack said, caution in his voice, hesitation in each syllable. A wise approach, given Henry wielded the kind of power the Druid dreamed of, but would never control. "You'll keep your word to me?"

"Which one do you want?"

"Won't know until I meet them."

"Nicole will be less trouble."

The Druid huffed. "Then I want Cate."

"So be it." Reaching the bottom of the hill, Henry moved into the shadowy confines of the forest. "Forty-eight hours, Tamarack. Do not disappoint me."

The Druid bowed his head in reverence.

Henry nodded, accepting his due, then with a murmur, deployed his magic. A pop sounded. Stardust rushed over his skin. A moment later, he dematerialized, becoming nothing but a scramble of molecules, dreaming of dead dragons and healthy heirs as he traveled into the Grampian Mountains toward his new home.

ALSO BY COREENE CALLAHAN

Dragonfury Scotland

Fury of a Highland Dragon

Fury of Shadows

Fury of Denial

Fury of Persuasion

Fury of Isolation

Fury of Frustration

Fury of Misfortune

"Villains" of the Dragonfury Series

Fury of Fate

Fury of Conviction

Dragonfury Series

Fury of Fire

Fury of Ice

Fury of Seduction

Fury of Desire

Fury of Obsession

Fury of Surrender

Fury of Destruction

Fury of Aggression

Circle of Seven Series

Knight Awakened

Knight Avenged

Warriors of the Realm Series

Warrior's Revenge

ABOUT THE AUTHOR

Coreene Callahan is the best-selling author of the Dragon-fury Novels and Circle of Seven Series, in which she combines her love of romance and adventure with her passion for history. After graduating with honors in psychology and taking a detour to work in interior design, Coreene returned to her first love: writing. Her debut novel, *Fury of Fire*, was a finalist in the New Jersey Romance Writers Golden Leaf Contest in two categories: Best First Book and Best Paranormal. She lives in Canada with her family, a spirited Anatolian Shepherd, and her wild imaginary world.

9 781648 394522